Misunderstood
. . . by a Single Twist of Fate

C.C. Graham

authorHOUSE®

AuthorHouse™
1663 Liberty Drive
Bloomington, IN 47403
www.authorhouse.com
Phone: 1-800-839-8640

First published by AuthorHouse   01/09/2012

ISBN: 978-1-4567-6245-2 (sc)
ISBN: 978-1-4567-6246-9 (ebk)

Library of Congress Control Number: 2011907279

Printed in the United States of America

Any people depicted in stock imagery provided by Thinkstock are models, and such images are being used for illustrative purposes only. Certain stock imagery © Thinkstock.

This book is printed on acid-free paper.

Contents

Acknowledgements

I thank first and foremost, the reason I am even here, God. I thank my motivator for everything I do, my Grandmother, Mama. To my parents, thank you for your total support.

Special thanks to my Editor Phillip J. Matheson for taking me through this entire process.

To my siblings, Christal for actually sitting and listening to me read my story to her and my brother for his moral support.

Thanks also to my other family members including aunties Helen, Margaret and Wendy for simply being awesome.

To special friends such as Marie Bhagan, Monique Mitchell, Candice Roberts, Arianne Kennedy and Aryana Mohammed I give my heartfelt thanks for your encouragement.

And last but certainly not least I thank my muse Tiffany Michelle Blair who has been with me from the very beginning of this story.

For
Olivia A. Gooding and her beautiful son Shem
Thanks for the inspiration.

And I thought my life was a mess . . .

Well it was, but it just looked perfect compared to his. He had it worse off than me, much worse . . .

October 7—Sunday

My hair briefly covered my vision of the screen before me as the wind blew. I wasted no time in tucking the fly away strand behind my ear, before focusing my eyes on the words that appeared on the screen. I laughed at the reply and quickly typed something back. I pulled up the temporarily forgotten window as I awaited another reply.

This was pretty much the highlight of my life. I would talk to my cyber friends whom I hadn't ever met in person, under my favorite tree in the private field a block from my house. Why I would waste my time talking to cyber people when I had real friends, you might be asking. Well I would be if I had any real friends. It's not like I choose not to have friends. Of course not, I really wish I had some, but being the naturally shy person that I am it was extremely out of character for me to approach a person.

My name is Brooklynn Vladimir. No, I am not Russian; my last name just originates there. I have short, wavy black hair and unnaturally large brown eyes. I think that is why people tend to stay away from me, because of my eyes, hence the reason I detest them so much, the other reason being that I inherited them from my father . . . I'll explain that later. I went to the closest high school to my house which happens to be public and I was almost seventeen years old. My birthday is December 8th. I guess that about sums it up for me, I'm not much, sorry if I disappoint.

Every day after school and all day on weekends and holidays I would escape to my haven under this huge willow tree I am currently sitting under at the moment. Most of the time, I would be occupied by my laptop. It was the most prized possession I owned, because on the internet I could be anyone I wanted to be, yet could still be myself and it was the only place that I was accepted. I practically lived in that abandoned field and it was quite alright, because no one else comes there and my mom doesn't have a problem with it.

But as the day turned to dusk which inevitably turned into nightfall, I would always be hesitant to make my way back home. And it was no exception when the sky faded to black that night. I hesitantly shut off my personal heaven and began making my way home as slowly as I could possibly go without appearing to any passersby that my legs were fighting a battle against each other.

I dragged myself up the pathway to the front door and opened it with my key before stepping inside. I locked it again before turning to go upstairs.

I opened my door and walked straight over to my desk to put the computer back to charge, before grabbing a change of clothes and walking into my adjacent bathroom. I felt unbearably monotonous as I opened the faucets and turned it to the right temperature. I always did this, everyday was the same old routine and I had gotten fed up of it a long time ago, but what could I do? Runaway? Right . . . as if I had anywhere better to go.

I couldn't be bothered to stay up, that night because it was a Monday the following morning and I would have to attend school. I slipped into bed after I turned off the lights and fell asleep a few minutes later.

October 8—Monday

Beep-Beep-Beep-Beep-Be-

I flipped open my phone and shut off its alarm, just to turn over in bed with the intention of drifting back to sleep. I had gone to sleep early, but no amount of sleep could ever make me willing to attend school. Sadly, the alarm just returned a few minutes later, which snatched my last chance to fall back into blissful sleep. I groaned this time flipping over and sitting upright at the edge of my bed.

Great here we go again . . .

I pulled a t-shirt and jeans from my closet before making my way to the bathroom to relieve myself and do the usual morning routine. Twenty five minutes later I emerged with a white t-shirt supporting the converse slogan and a pair of faded jeans. I slipped on my favorite pair of Vans before heading out my door.

I walked downstairs to see my mother with a cup of coffee sitting at the table reading something. For some reason still unknown to me I ventured to greet her.

"Morning," I said softly but it was clearly audible.

I wasn't surprised when she made no signs of acknowledging me. It's not like she ever did, and today wasn't any different. I sighed and went to the fridge.

When I said I thought my life was messed up it was because of this. So sixteen years ago, my thirty year old mother, was raped by my dad. This made her fourteen when it happened. She got pregnant and since her family didn't believe in abortions, she was forced to keep me, much to her dismay. You see, her family had wealthy ties so she was educated finely thus having no problems with dropping out of school like most do. Well actually she was taken out of school, but was tutored by one of the best teachers so other than being emotionally scarred; the pregnancy didn't really affect her life. She never had to take care of me either, because her parents hired nannies and babysitters for me while she lived life like she always did.

As you can see though, she dislikes me . . . a lot. See, she had a vision

of what her life was supposed to be like since she was young. She was going to be a successful lawyer with a loving husband living in the perfect house with no annoying kids to look after. Apparently when I was conceived I ruined it all and she makes it clear to me every day when she shows no feelings of affection to her only daughter. If I had the choice I wouldn't have chosen to be born either, but life, unfortunately, for me, doesn't operate that way.

I threw an apple into my bag for lunch before leaving the house and my bitter mother.

I slowly began the journey to school. I could take all the time I wanted seeing as I was half an hour early anyway. As I reached the main road, I saw other kids walking to school, all of them with a friend, laughing and smiling in the presence of someone who cared for them. I envied my whole school, everyone in that place had someone they could go to; there were cliques everywhere. Even the loners and outcasts as some called them had their own little group that they retired to. I wish I could be one of them, laughing with other people who had something in common with me, but I didn't, and I was used to it by now. I merely scanned them from afar as they walked aimlessly towards the school.

But out of all the people and cliques there was one group of people that caught my eye as they walked, blissfully ignorant, ahead of me. There were three of them and they were all boys, all clad in black, with fringes covering their eyes and streaks of color throughout their perfectly styled hair; typical emo. I don't exercise the use of label for people, but it was easier to call them that seeing that I only knew their names; Ajay Edison, Dakota Richards and Tristan Jacobs.

Why would they catch my attention? Well maybe it was the fact that they were all popular within the school's community and all of them were hot. They had girls fawning over them and even I will grudgingly admit that they have been the cause for that annoying flurry of butterflies in the pit of my stomach whenever I was close to any of them. They were hot, popular and undeniably badass. They had confidence and an attractive air of arrogance that just drew people, especially girls, to them. And I was no exception.

I sighed in frustration as I caught myself staring at them. I shook my head clearing my thoughts and headed towards the school. I went straight for the library as soon as I put my things away in my locker. School wasn't due to start until half eight and it was now five past eight. I picked up a book and buried myself in it until the fateful bell decided to commence yet another day. As expected the bell rang right at the scheduled time which meant I replaced the book and headed to homeroom. I slipped in and made my way to the back of the room to sit in a corner desk. I drummed my fingers silently on the desk's surface as I tuned out the voice of a chirpy teacher talking about the weekend.

The bell rang again signaling my cue to leave for my first class which was Art. I relaxed a little as I grabbed my notepad from my locker knowing that Art was going to be the best subject I would endure today. I walked in right before the teacher did and once again made it to the back of the room.

"I see you are all bright and awake this Monday morning . . ." he continued, but I tuned him out until he reached the part about the assignment we were supposed to do for the day.

"Since you have already given up your portfolio last Thursday I think it would be fair if I gave you some free time for this period."

More free time . . . great.

I sighed and took out my sketch pad deciding that I would doodle or do something on my own.

Finally after calculus, lunch came which wasn't all that better, because I usually sat outside, alone or sometimes ended up eating in the Art room. And since I wasn't in the mood to watch couples make out behind the school, I grabbed my apple and made my way back to the Art room. No one else was present so I eased up and went to a window seat to occupy myself with watching floating clouds to pass the time away.

After eating my apple I was lost in an intense daydream and didn't notice when someone entered the classroom. It seemed that the person didn't see me either because he was too caught up in his own world as well. The way the classroom was, with objects and sculptures scattered artfully all over, it was easy to be obscured by something. So when I woke from my trance like state, I still ceased to notice the other being. As I was about to get up and stretch my legs I heard a frustrated grunt coming from the other side of the room which caused me to yelp unexpectedly. The person heard it and in a few moments he was up and watching me with apprehension and confusion. It was none other than the, most wanted and hottest guy in school belonging to that clique I mentioned earlier.

"Who are you?" he asked probably thinking I was new since he knew pretty much everyone in the school.

But before I could answer, he fired another question.

"What are you doing here?" he asked eyeing me suspiciously as if I were an alien, as if I hadn't been coming here every day to eat lunch.

I suddenly felt out of place as he asked these questions, although I was given permission by the Art teacher to have lunch in here. I was not one to stand up to other people so I bowed my head, mumbled something incoherent and moved passed him for the door. I was about to open the door when his voice rang out again.

"Wait!" but I had ignored his command, not wanting to be confronted, and quickly slipped out of the classroom and into the hall.

By the time I had made it to the bathroom a few hallways over; my cheeks were flustered, not from getting there, but because of the situation I had been in. A hot guy talked to me, it had never happened before and I wasn't too eager for it to happen again. I had no experience with people in person, let alone boys.

Glad that's over. I'll probably never encounter him again and he will have forgotten already, so it's good.

I spent the rest of my lunch period in a bathroom stall and almost fell asleep if it wasn't for the annoying ringing of the school bell. I leaned off the stall's wall and left the bathroom after making sure I carried no signs of sleep on my face.

I still had three more periods to endure after lunch and neither of them were worthy of my time, so I'll skip ahead to after school.

I made it home in record time of five minutes. My mother was hardly ever home when I was so I went straight to my room, showered and threw on some clothes while unplugging my laptop and putting it into its case.

Like always I could be seen by all the people on the way between my house and my hideout. Like I said, this was routine for me, almost every day I could be found in that field with my laptop under that aging willow tree.

It's odd how my butt hasn't left any imprints in the ground from the countless times I have stationed myself there. This time as I plunked down in the same spot, I didn't boot up my laptop right away. Instead I sat there slowly drifting off and getting lost in a daydream while I temporarily forgot it at my side.

It's amazing, the places my imagination took me to in my otherwise unoccupied mind. It was so amazing in fact that I was totally oblivious to the figure standing just a few hundred yards away, watching me intently with curiosity residing in their eyes.

When I awoke from my daydream, the person had already left, leaving me in complete ignorance of the unknown being.

I sighed and pulled the machine onto my lap before booting it up and immediately logging onto an Instant Messenger where some of my 'friends' were already appearing online as well. I smiled and began to make use of the time I had left that evening.

October 9—Tuesday

Walking to school was a daze for me as I thought about what would happen later that day. My mother was going out of town for 'business' and I would have the whole house to myself and that was saying something, because the house I lived in was one of the biggest in this already expensive neighborhood. Besides the income that my mother received, her family was, as I mentioned before, wealthy.

It was also supposed to rain today so it was obvious I wouldn't be able to go to my sanctuary, but that was all well since my mother wouldn't be home anyway.

School went by as usual except for lunch.

The bell rang so, as expected everyone rushed to the cafeteria to get to their food and friends. Since I hadn't felt like eating lunch and the Art room was being used for a staff meeting I decided I would just go to the bathroom and spend the rest of lunch there.

Upon entering I was greeted with hushed sobs, which made me feel like turning around and hightailing out of there, but on second thought I realized I had nowhere else to go and the person was in a stall and wouldn't see me anyway.

I went in hesitantly heading straight for a stall of my own when a door on my side flung open. I nearly screamed, nearly. I looked up and caught the sight of a teary eyed red head.

"Um, sorry you had to see me like this," she said softly as she brushed past me to wash her face in the sink.

That was weird, normally someone would insult me on sight in this school yet this girl didn't do that, she apologized. I suddenly felt a sense of empathy towards the poor girl as I realized she wasn't one of those cold hearted bitches that roamed the halls of this confused school.

"Um, it's ok," I said, and boy that felt weird.

I can't remember the last time I spoke to another person besides my mother and grandparents. I wasn't a mute or anything, it's just that I never had the opportunity to talk to anyone and the teachers never bothered to call on me in class so I had little opportunity there either.

She smiled with puffy eyes as she looked up at me. I took this as a welcome to say more or at least a sign that she didn't hate me.

"Uh, what's your name?" I asked for lack of anything better to say.

"Jamie," she said sniffling softly.

"I'm Brooklynn," I offered.

She only nodded her head slightly and I took that as an indication that she had heard me. I became silent again as I had nothing else to say, but didn't have to say anything as she spoke up.

"I know I have only now met you and everything, but could I ask you for a favor?" she asked me with a soft pleading glint in her eyes.

"Um, well what is it?" I asked curiously as to what she could possibly want from me, probably to go to the office and ask for her to go home or something.

"C-could you, um, skip the next class with me?" she asked adding quickly, "all my friends have abandoned me and I really need someone right now, please?"

I was shocked that she would actually ask that of me.

Not the skipping part, but the part where she wanted me for company.

This was the first time since before I could remember when someone ever wanted my presence.

Looking at my expression she dropped her gaze and said, "I would understand if you don't want to, I'm sorry I shouldn't have asked th-" I cut her off before she could continue.

"Wait, yes, I'll come with you, it's okay," I said.

She looked up at me with a small smile, "Thank you so much," she said right as the bell, ending our lunch, screeched.

She dried off her face with a paper towel before we both proceeded to the well known fire escape.

You see, our school authorities are really cheap, either that or they are really slack and I personally think it's both. There was a fire escape at the side of the school that wasn't working like it should, it didn't lock from the inside or trigger any alarms like normal ones. So as you may have already guessed, it was a really good way for students to ditch school whenever they felt like it and they even used it to enter the school whenever they were running late as to not get caught. So naturally that was where Jamie and I were headed through the mass of students as lunch ended.

Right outside that door was the school field. Most of the ditchers hid behind the bleachers which were situated right next to the school so it was easy to dash across to it without getting seen by teachers from their classroom windows.

It seems that we were the only delinquents that day because the infamous spot behind the bleachers was void of any students.

We sat and got comfy in our selected spots under the bleachers. The first period after lunch went by with Jamie and me getting acquainted with each other. I learned that she was a sweet sixteen year old girl with a humorous and free spirit. It was refreshing and liberating to talk to someone about everything and anything. Around second period she decided that I was trustworthy enough to let me in on why I had met her in such a state in the bathroom which was also the reason why her friends had abandoned her.

"I was at my boyfriend's house a few weeks ago," she had mentioned to me about her boyfriend when we were getting to know each other, "we were watching a movie, he had called me over because he was feeling lonely since his parents had gone to an overnight party on the other side of town. So anyway we were just watching the movie when we started to kiss, and it eventually turned to a heated make-out session, you know how these things happened right, and before I knew it we're undressing in his room."

Actually I had no idea how a kiss turned into a make out session because I had never made out with a boy before let alone kissed one. I was a pure virgin and apparently she had never before had sex either I learned as she continued.

"It was the first time I ever had sex, he took my virginity," while she was telling me all this though, I still couldn't see the relevance to what this had to do with her crying in the bathroom at lunch or have her friends leave her, this I found out as she continued.

"And in the heat of it all, we forgot to use protection . . ." at this point I could figure out the rest of the story, but I stayed silent and let her go on, "I found out a week ago that I was pregnant," she paused waiting to see if I would do anything and when I didn't that seemed to please her 'cause she went on, "I'm too afraid to tell him though, and I don't know what to do, but no matter what I will not have an abortion."

By this time she was back to tears, leaning into me. It was awkward at first since this was my first experience with someone crying on my shoulder, but I began to stroke her back and I told her it was ok. That seemed to calm her down after a while so I figured I must be doing something right. After about ten minutes of sitting there with Jamie soaking my hoodie, my legs began to cramp from sitting on that one position, luckily though she sat up and dried her eyes.

"Thank you Brooklynn," she said smiling at me with blue agonized, tainted eyes.

Although I had only known Jamie for a short while she was the only person in my sixteen years of existence that had treated me with such kindness.

"It's okay, and I will always be here for you," I offered whole heartedly meaning it.

"That means a lot to me," she said, "and I can tell we're going to be great friends," she said smiling.

It was my turn to smile; she had no idea how much that meant to *me*.

Before we knew it, students were pouring out of the entrance of the school's building.

We both stood up and headed back into the school through the fire escape to get our bags from our lockers, before making our way outside.

She turned to me, "Brooklynn, can I get your number so I can call you tonight?" she asked.

"Sure," I said slipping my hand into my pocket for my cell phone.

We exchanged them and punched our numbers in, saved them and handed the devices back to their respective owners.

"I'll call you tonight, okay?" she said as we made it to the end of the parking lot.

"Okay," I said as she pulled me in for a hug.

She pulled away and turned left as I turned right. We both turned back after a few steps to see the other stupidly grinning from ear to ear.

I turned around and happy for the first time in my life made my way home. I couldn't stop smiling as I entered the empty house. I had made a friend today.

A real friend, who accepted me for who I am, she was nice, caring and everything a person could want in a friend.

I actually skipped up the stairs as I made my way to my room. I even forgot about my earlier dismay about not going to my place of sanity. I stripped, showered and changed. Then I bounced my way downstairs to grab a bite to eat. As I was getting ready to take a bite out of my cheese sandwich the doorbell's chimes resonated off the walls of the house. I grunted and put my succulent sandwich down as I made my way to the door.

This had better be good. Who could it be anyway? My mother was smart enough to allow all her colleagues over when I was not around, so that was crossed off the list of possible people. It was most likely a sales person trying to sell something, since I never had any visitors.

I opened the door and almost fainted from shock when it turned out to be the hottest guy at school, my crush, the guy who I had encountered in the Art room yesterday, Ajay Edison. I regained my composure and the confusion set in as to why the most popular guy at school would be at my house.

"Hi, you're Brooklynn, right?" he asked as he eyed me.

I had to grip the door slightly as I heard him say my name; it was so sexy coming from his mouth that I just wanted him to say it over and over again, preferably in a candlelit room while music was playing softly in the background.

"Yes?" I sounded like I wasn't sure myself.

"Can I speak to you?" he asked.

What? Why would you want to speak to me?!

"Uh," was the only thing I could muster.

"Well, if you are busy right now, maybe I can do it tomorrow after school," he said.

I automatically nodded my head. He thanked me and left. I closed the door and went back into the kitchen. Only when I was about to take the first bite of my neglected sandwich did I realize what I had gotten myself into.

Holy shit!! The hottest guy at school just came to my house asking to talk to me. Why the hell did I say yes? I am so stupid! What have I gotten myself into? Now I am going to humiliate myself in front of him . . . wait, why did he want to talk to me anyway? OMG!!! Aaahhhh!!!

Once again I neglected my sandwich at the table as I went upstairs to my room, I flopped on my bed and my mind began to wonder why Ajay would want to talk to me. It just didn't make sense. He was sexy and hot and let's face it; I was just plain and not.

He had black, probably dyed, hair that was styled so it hung loosely in his face covering one of his eyes and sometimes both. The back was choppy and short, in that new trendy haircut. He had gorgeous green eyes, a perfectly slender nose that led to sexy lips that almost every girl at my school wanted desperately to kiss. What made his lips so inviting was his trademark snakebite piercing.

I began to entertain myself with the farfetched idea that he was madly in love with me and was going to profess his love to me. Maybe he would get down on his knee and ask me to be his girlfriend, or maybe he would take me to a beautiful lake where we would watch the sunset together where he would then propose his undying love to me. The third, consisting of him and I riding in a Ferrari into the distance was cut short as the phone's ringing shattered my thoughts. I couldn't stay irritated though as I checked the Caller ID. It was Jamie calling like she said she would.

We ended up talking all night until her mom scolded her for being on the phone for so long.

We said our goodbyes sometime after eleven. I was so exhausted. I had never talked that much over the phone, and my ear was numb from having the receiver pressed up against it. Strangely enough I did not mention the encounter with Ajay; I was way too occupied with her rambling on about random topics to remember. I wasn't yet ready to go to bed so I went to my TV and turned it on out of boredom. The first channel I flipped to was the weather channel. To my surprise and delight it stated that the continuous rain that had been happening all of that evening was leading to a huge storm that was supposed to take place tonight. As if on cue a loud peal of thunder rolled throughout the overcast sky.

I turned the channel hoping that the storm would be big and strong enough to force schools to close. I flopped onto my queen sized canopy bed and leaned against my satin covered pillows as I sighed in comfort. I had a strange love for rainstorms. I found them to be calming. I usually read a book or did something palliative in the comforts of my room whenever there was a storm raging outside, I even considered it better than going to the field.

I lazily flipped through the channels and finding nothing better to watch, switched off the television. I jumped out of bed, suddenly feeling hungry again and went downstairs. As I turned into the kitchen a flash of lightening illuminated the whole room and I saw that I had left my sandwich on the counter from earlier. It almost looked creepy the way the lightning flashed like that, like the sandwich wanted its revenge because I didn't eat it. I picked up the plate and placed it in the fridge and walked over to the cupboard to look for snacks.

One of the pros of being loaded is that one never runs out of food or entertainment. This was the case as I opened the overhead door and had to catch a few bags of chips that came tumbling out. I hopped onto the counter on my knees to get a better view and ended up with a bag of Ripples and another of chocolate covered pretzels. I hopped down and went back to the fridge to get a dip for my chips.

Only minutes later I was sitting on my bed with the bags of food opened at my side while I watched a movie. The rain and thunder was still raging outside and once or twice the lights had flickered. I wasn't at all worried, I had no problem with the dark and we had a generator anyway. I was actually subconsciously egging the storm on and hoping that it would be stronger by tomorrow and that I would have a perfect excuse not to attend school. If there were no school I wouldn't have to deal with Ajay. Simple.

I fell asleep before the credits of the movie even came on.

October 10—Wednesday

Beep—beep—beep—beep

The most annoying sound of my morning alarm woke me up at the crack of another morning. I rolled over in bed only to fall off and land in a crumpled and tangled heap of blankets on the carpeted floor. I moaned and was about to go back to sleep when a loud boom resonated off the walls. My head shot up in alarm. The look of fright slipped off my face as I glanced out the window and caught sight of the dark, grey sky.

Yay, it was still a raging storm outside. I untangled myself as I got to my feet and stumbled over to the window. It was difficult to see further than a few feet in front of me, because the rain was so heavy, but I could distinguish a fallen tree a few yards down the road from my house.

Excellent, I had the perfect excuse not to attend school that morning and if they were to call I could easily say that a tree had fallen in front of my house. Well technically it fell in front of my neighbor's house, but who's coming to verify that? Certainly not the school board. Easy as pie. What is so easy about pie? I don't know, but who am I to mess with such a traditionally used quip?

I threw my blankets back onto my bed and made my way to my adjacent bathroom to take a hot shower. As the water pellets massaged my back I couldn't help but think of Jamie . . . (Ok that sounded beyond wrong.) Maybe I should go to school today so I could see her. I decided to call her instead and see if she was going to school. With that thought in mind I rinsed of all the soap suds and jumped out of the shower. I wrapped a towel around me and grabbed my phone, punching in her number. It connected after three rings.

"Yellow," she said into the speaker.

"Hey Jamie this is Brooklynn, you going to school today?" I asked her.

"No way, my mom wouldn't let me," she said sounding amused.

Suddenly a thought sprung into my head. And I had to jump on the opportunity.

"Um, can you make it to my house then?" I asked her hopefully.

"Let me ask my mom, maybe she'll drop me on her way to work," she said and I could hear her talking to someone else in the background before hearing an excited squeal. She put the phone back to her ear.

"She said she'll drop me off on her way to work," she explained.

"Ok, I'll see you then?" I verified.

"Yeah, bye!" she sang and the click could be heard as the line went dead.

I flipped my phone closed and put it back onto my side table only then noticing I was dripping and still had a towel around me. I dried myself off and went into my closet where I pulled on a comfortable t-shirt and a pair of cargo pants. The floor downstairs would no doubt be freezing, so I pulled on my fuzzy, bunny rabbit bedroom slippers after I spotted them at the foot of my bed. I had a feeling Jamie wouldn't care if I wore them so I felt comfortable doing so.

Not more than a few minutes later I heard the ringing of my doorbell, I ran from the living room to answer it. Before I could even say anything a blur of red and yellow knocked me off my feet.

"I am so cold!" she exclaimed as she hugged me tightly.

And I could see why, the wind was howling fiercely and the rain was biting and chilly. I waved to her mom as she drove off. I closed the door and turned to a shivering Jamie. Her hair was stuck in wet strands across her face. I took her bright yellow raincoat and hung it in the coat closet in the entrance foyer.

"Your house is huge," she said with awe as she gazed around her.

"Yeah, I guess," no reason in denying the obvious truth.

I motioned for her to follow me into the kitchen.

"Did you have breakfast yet? Do you want anything?" I asked going towards the fridge and opening it looking for something to drink for myself.

"Yeah, thanks," she said.

"Well go ahead, take anything you'd like, help yourself," I offered sweeping my hand to further gesture what I said.

"You sure?" she asked shyly.

"Mi casa es su casa," I recited as I went to one of the bar stools and sat with my glass of orange juice.

"Well ok," she said sounding hyped.

"Can I cook something?" she asked unsure of herself a few moments later, pulling her head out of the fridge.

"Yeah, go ahead, I'll wash the dishes if you cook something good," I said grinning hoping that it would lighten her up a bit.

People always felt intimidated whenever they walked into my house.

Maybe it's because it was so pristine. Or maybe it was the empty and strict aura that lingered.

This whole friend thing was great. It felt odd at first because instead of talking to friends that I couldn't see, there was someone right in front of me. It was easy really, just no typing.

She went to the fridge and searched through it before emerging with a pack of bacon and a carton of eggs. She rested them on the counter and brought out a block of cheese.

"Bacon and eggs?" she asked.

"Sure," I said shrugging as I watched her arrange the stuff she needed for making breakfast.

A few laugh filled minutes later she was standing over the pan with my mother's frilly pink apron on and a spatula in her hand.

I was now sitting on top of the counter near the stove talking to her while she cooked us breakfast.

I found myself telling her things I never told anyone. How I felt at times, my interests, what my life was like, who my mother was, the story of my birth and not once did she look at me differently, she even shared some of her own stories. I was so comfortable with talking to her, she was so loving and fun it was hard not to be.

"So he just left her?" she asked incredulously as she rearranged the food sizzling away in the skillet.

"Yes, he raped her. I don't think the protocol is to wait around and make sure their victim is alright," I answered sarcastically knowing she wouldn't take offense.

"Didn't she call the police and report it though?" she inquired lowering the heat on the stove.

"She said it happened in a dark alley way and all she could see were his eyes, they were big and brown, like mine," I replied again.

"Oh," she said as she focused once more on our bacon and eggs.

Talking about births, the thought of her giving birth sprung to my mind and I ventured to ask a question.

"I don't mean to be nosy, but did you tell your mother?" I asked knowing that she knew what I was referring to.

"Yeah, strangely enough she was ecstatic, she hopes it's a boy since she always wanted one, but she doesn't agree with me in the part where I don't tell my boyfriend," she said shrugging.

She still hadn't mentioned to me who the father-to-be was so I was guessing it was a person that I wouldn't know, or didn't go to our school or wasn't even in our town. I brushed it off knowing that she wasn't ready to divulge the guy's identity so I let it slide.

We ended up eating in my room on the carpet. She didn't want to eat on the bed for fear of dirtying anything. I also agreed because I had my sheets changed recently and didn't want to get grease on the satin. It was a bitch to get out. We sat and ate just talking about everything and anything in general when she accidentally spilled orange juice on her shirt from laughing too hard.

"Oh crap," she said as the juice spilled.

"Don't worry you can wear one of mine," I said helping her from the ground and going towards my closet.

"Really? Th-" she stopped short as she entered my closet behind me.

"Whoa!" she half whispered, "This is amazing."

I laughed at her expression.

"Thanks," I said walking further into the closet.

"I mean I knew you were rich, but this is just . . . wow," she trailed off as she gazed around her with a glazed look in her eyes.

She was referring to the size. It was big, about half the size of my room and my room was already large. That and everything was color coordinated. As we walked down the aisle, the racks above held tops arranged in color and style, while the bottom rack held pants also arranged the same way.

On the other side of the isle, the left side, the top held dresses and the bottom held skirts. At the end of the isle the entire wall was covered in rows upon rows of color coordinated footwear. From heels to flats to sneakers and almost any style of shoe you can think of.

I was proud to say that my closet resembled that of a rock star's. Although one would never guess considering the plain tees and jeans I usually wore to school, those I just took from the dresser in my room. I hardly used the clothes in here anyway. I had no one to impress.

I sat on a footstool and I watched her admire my clothes and shoes. It was comical to see her stop and gush over one thing, then get sidetracked by another.

"Ready to pick something now?" I asked amused at her unwavering awe.

"What? Oh, um, yeah," she said as she was brought back from her high.

"Ok, so I think we wear the same size, go ahead and pick something out" I said.

"From where?" she asked.

"Anywhere?" I said unsure of what she meant.

"Eee! I love you Brooklynn, really!" she exclaimed in bewilderment.

"Yeah," I said now smiling also.

Unknown to her, that was the first time I had ever heard anyone other than my grandparents say those words to me. She may not have realized what she said, but it meant the world to me and I found myself caring for this girl more and more.

She hugged me and began her search. A few minutes later she came to me with a cute long sleeved top, the one that I had gotten from Paris last Christmas. I've never been anywhere near France, but my mother has a designer friend who doesn't have a sixteen year old daughter of her own to shop for.

I nodded and she squealed in delight and ran to the bathroom to put it on. It amused me how she acted around clothes and accessories. She was the ultimate girl, like the ones I had seen on T.V all the time. It made me feel good the way she thanked me when she came back out wearing the top.

"No problem, you can borrow it anytime, it looks better on you anyway," I said taking her stained shirt and tossing it in my hamper.

"You are the greatest friend I could ever have," she said hugging me as we walked out of the closet.

"Thank you," I said and I really meant it.

The rest of the day we spent laughing and talking about our lives. She lived with her mom, had an older sister who was away at college and had a dog, but her sister had taken him with her. Then she told me that she had told her friends about her getting preggers, but they all abandoned her.

That was truly vicious for her so called friends to do, how could they just leave her like that in her most vulnerable moment? That was beyond me, but I knew that I would not turn out to be like her friends. Her friendship meant a lot to me and I would always be there for her if I could.

Then she started about her boyfriend.

"Too bad we broke up," she went on to say and it caught my attention.

From what she had told me so far I thought they were still together, I mean she never called him her ex.

"You did?" I asked.

"Yeah, the spark just wasn't there anymore after we had sex, so we separated on good terms," she informed me, "well except it was good terms until I found out I got pregnant. I sort of avoided him since then."

"Oh," I nodded and she continued on.

One topic shifted to the next and soon before we even knew it, it was seven o' clock, time for her mother to come pick her up.

I told her she could keep the top when she told me she would bring it back for me tomorrow and I smiled at her obvious appreciation. Since it was still raining heavily she had to hurry to the waiting car.

That night I went to sleep to light, smile-filled dreams. This was tuning out to be the best week of my life, it was like a turning point, where everything just starts turning around for the better.

October 11—Thursday

My mother was still out of town and I was tempted to stay home from school again, but the storm had passed just leaving light showers and overcast skies. I sat in bed for a while deciding whether or not to go to school when my cell phone disturbed my decision making.

I flipped it open and read the text from Jamie asking if I was going to school today. I decided that I would since I had nothing better to do all day at home except surf the net which was becoming less and less entertaining to me. I texted back with my reply and got out of bed to get ready.

Just a little while later caught me grabbing an apple and getting ready to leave. My walk to school was uneventful except for the part where Ajay had spotted me and gave me a meaningful look.

Crap, he still remembers the other day. I'll just have to avoid him, no problem there.

I met Jamie by my locker before class started and we just made small talk before the bell rang separating us for the day, except for lunch.

I had no problem trying to avoid Ajay as the day went by because he had none of my classes either, but lunch time I sort of feared a little. Fortunately for me Jamie didn't want to sit in the cafeteria because she felt uncomfortable with all the new dislike from her ex-friends. So we both ended up behind the bleachers, the same place we had been in the day before yesterday. The grass was dry due to the fact that the stands above sheltered it from the rain.

"Brooklynn, I just want to let you know that I won't be here for the rest of the day."

I stopped mid bite with my apple still in my mouth, I had to take it out to speak, "What, why?"

"My mom is taking me to the doctor for a check-up to make sure everything is alright," she said referring to the life form gradually growing inside her.

I was disappointed, but I totally understood the situation so I didn't say anything except, "Well call me when you get back, and tell me what happened, ok?"

21

"Of course, but it's just some tests to make sure I am healthy enough to support the baby while it's growing," she said taking a bite out of her sandwich.

Lunch had ended and I was feeling a little down since Jamie had left right before the lunch bell rang.

By the time school was dismissed I was anxious to get home so I could be free from school. I had turned onto my route home and was walking at a casual pace when I heard footsteps behind me. This was different as I was usually the only person on this route from school. When I found the courage to turn around my eyes went wide as I saw who the footsteps belonged to. I whipped my head back around and was about to speed up when a hand suddenly wrapped around the crook of my elbow forcing me to be whipped right back around to face Ajay Edison.

"I need to talk to you," he said staring determinedly down at me.

"Now?" I asked shyly looking down.

"Yes, why are you busy?" he asked sarcastically.

"Well . . . I-"

"Good, come on," he interrupted me and pulled me in the other direction.

"Where are we going?" I asked bewildered as to why he was leading me somewhere completely unknown to me.

"My place," he answered briefly, letting go of my hand and expecting me to follow him, which I stupidly did.

"Why?!" I asked.

It was beyond me why he would need to talk to me at his house.

"It's going to rain soon," he answered.

I looked up and indeed the sky held the promise of imminent rain.

We made it to his house in silence after that, me mostly wondering why the hell I was still following him and what on earth he could possibly want to talk to me about.

He unlocked the door and walked inside. I expected to see someone from his family, but as we walked past the living room and into the kitchen I was surprised to find it empty.

"Is anyone else here?" I asked suddenly feeling uncomfortable with the idea of being all alone with Ajay Edison, ultimate badass.

"No," he said indifferently as he opened the fridge and pulled out a can of Sprite.

"Want anything?" he asked turning to me.

I shook my head no as I had instantly lost my voice. I felt unsafe and out of character all of a sudden.

He leaned against the counter at the other side of the kitchen with the can of Sprite in one hand while he stared curiously at me.

I began to feel uneasy and shifted under his scrutinizing stare yet he still didn't avert his eyes and I snapped.

"What?" it came out soft yet demanding.

That didn't faze him though as he still stared at me.

"Why don't you ever sit in the cafeteria?" he asked still staring.

That was not what I expected to hear. I don't know what I expected, but it definitely wasn't that.

"That's what you drag me all the way to your house to find out?" I asked slightly irritated because I knew that wasn't what he intended to talk about.

He simply stood there waiting for my answer. This was beginning to get annoying. I waited for the reason why I was even there to surface, but still he made no move to answer me.

I spun on my heels and left the kitchen heading straight for the front door. I yanked it open and walked outside to begin my journey home.

I sat on my bed as my mind drifted. Jamie hadn't called yet and my mind had slithered to earlier that evening.

I can't believe I followed him in the first place. Obviously it was a joke; he must have been forced by his friends as a twisted dare or something to do that, now I am going to be the laughing stock at school.

I was suddenly angry at him, but then became angry with myself for letting myself believe he would actually want to talk to me.

At around ten Jamie called telling me that everything was ok, but she had to go for weekly check-ups from now on. She asked me if she missed any gossip that might have taken place in school and I answered no. Jamie was more into the high school drama than I was.

After talking to her, around half past eleven I began to get ready for bed since tomorrow was another day of school and thankfully the last for the week. I fell asleep that night disappointed in myself of my actions earlier today.

October 12—Friday

I wasn't in the mood for going to school and I wasn't too keen on staying home either. So I reluctantly began to get ready for school after my second wakeup call from my phone.

During the walk to school that morning I kept my head down. I was sure that Ajay had told all his friends how I had naively followed him home. I walked briskly to my locker, got my Art pad and went to the library where I spent the rest of the time until school officially commenced.

Weeks past and Jamie and I became closer and closer, while every day I avoided Ajay, which didn't prove to be that hard since Jamie never wanted to sit in the cafeteria so I never appeared suspicious. His stares, whenever he walked by in the hallways were unnerving, because they were icy yet curious, but other than that that I never had the chance of running into him, thank God.

November 15—Wednesday

I had fifth period Science, but this time it was different because it included all the science students from the junior and senior year. I slipped into the gymnasium without being noticed and took a seat in the back of the crowd of talking students. Jamie was absent today due to an Ultrasound she had to take to see if the baby was coming along ok. So I was all alone with no one to talk to. I had opened up a bit since hanging around Jamie, but I was still shy. I had a few people that I talked to sometimes but that was it.

The students began to quiet down after the Science teacher, Mr. Dennis, walked to the front of the room.

"As you all know this is a joint class with all of my science students from juniors and seniors," a murmur of agreement could be heard before he continued again, "the reason for that is because I have decided that you will all be paired off to work on a project that you will all present to me at the end on the year."

Again the distinct murmur of the students' voices could be heard and quite frankly it was annoying me. Couldn't they just shut up and let the man finish? I wasn't in the greatest of moods and I wanted nothing more at the moment than for the day to end.

"Please be quiet while I read out the list of names," as he went down the list we all realized that it was a junior and a senior in each pair.

"Tristan Jacobs and Casey Lamarck,"

"Kayden Winston and Hailey Munroe,"

"Jamie Austin and Dakota Richards,"

I made sure to note that so I could inform her the next time I spoke to her.

"Ajay Edison and Brooklynn Vladimir,"

"Sasha Meadows and Brent Yale,"

I nearly choked on my own spit. WHAT!?!?

I was sure I had heard wrong, but when I looked at Ajay his smirk and resolute stare indicated that I wasn't having a nightmare.

Halfway through the period I asked one of the supervising teachers to use the bathroom with the intention of ditching the rest of the period because I had already gotten the information about the project I needed, but mostly because Ajay would not stop staring at me and it was annoying me whilst slightly creeping me out.

I had thought by the time a week had past he would have forgotten about the whole incident with his house and everything, but he never stopped staring at me with that cold, inquisitive expression and it was beyond me why he kept at it.

I strolled down the hallway leading to the fire escape, but decided against going outside since the weather was steadily becoming unbearably frigid since winter was nearing. Instead I turned the corner and began making my way to the band room on the third floor. The band room was only used for band practice which was on Thursdays and Tuesdays and was pretty much abandoned otherwise so it was a fitting place to go, and besides if any teacher were to walk in and confront me I could just tell them I had a study hall and that I used the time to practise. Practise what, I don't know. The only musical thing I know is where middle C is on piano.

I slipped in through the door and made my way to the back of the room where I sat down and began to doodle in my notebook. A scribble soon turned into a full page drawing of diverse things all collaged together. I was so absorbed in it that I didn't realize when the bell rang for the next period. I was so into the drawing in fact that when someone's voice broke my train of thought I dropped my pen virtually screaming from sheer fright.

But when I glanced up and into the face of the intruder, I really wanted to scream.

"Ditching class are we?" he said smirking down at me.

I didn't answer. I just glared up at him hoping that would be answer enough.

Why was it when I finally got away from him, I have to find out that I didn't?

I picked up my pen and went back to drawing, attempting to ignore him, but that was rather difficult as he was intently looking at me with those striking green eyes.

Leave, please leave.

I egged him on in my head, however instead of doing as I wished he walked over and sat down in front of me. I wanted to take my notebook and smack him with it. Hard. Why was he so persistent, and what the heck did he want from me? I thought the joke was over. Apparently I was wrong.

"I hope you took down notes, I was a bit busy," he said referring to our previous period and then I grudgingly recalled that I had to complete an entire science project with him.

He took my silence as his leeway to continue.

"I was thinking we could do it at my house-"

My head snapped up as I heard this.

"What? No-" I was cut off.

"Well then we'll just do it at yours, I'll come by around five," he said standing up with a satisfied smirk.

What? I never agreed to this. No you can't come over to my house. I don't want you there!!

I screamed in my head as I stood up also, annoyed at his manipulation.

"Or we could do it at school," I suggested quickly as he was about to turn around.

"We wouldn't have enough time," he said.

I tried to find a way out of this, but nothing intelligent came to my head quick enough.

"Or enough space," he said taking a step towards me which made me automatically walk back.

Before I could say anything else he spoke again.

"Because we need space," he said walking much closer which made me take another step back.

I *need space, back up dammit!*

"Or enough privacy," he said taking another step which resulted in me taking one back and having my back meet the unmistakable solidity of a wall.

He smirked and took a large stride forward bringing him directly in front of me; I could feel his breath fan across my face.

My skin heated up at the proximity and even more so when he slowly leaned towards me, his cheek brushed against mine as his hot breath tickled my ear.

"And we definitely need privacy," he whispered in my ear.

My breath hitched in my throat as he pulled away only to have his face hover about an inch from mine while he stared straight into my eyes. He pulled away, turned around and walked out of the music room.

I was left standing there like a blushing idiot.

What the hell just happened?

I snapped out of it when I remembered what he had said. He would be coming over to my house today. Crap! This was one time I wished my mother wasn't away on business trips so often. I was going to be alone in a house with Ajay. On the bright side it was my house. On the not so sunny side, that wouldn't stop him from being Ajay and that is what I feared most.

He held the title of the school's rebel for a reason. He had been to juvenile prison four times already; I didn't know what for, but I didn't want to find out either. He also was infamous for his tempers. He was known to do some pretty drastic things when he got pissed and let me tell you, he got pissed easily.

By the end of the day I was scared shitless of the possibility that I might get assaulted in my own home. How had I gotten myself into this?

This isn't my fault; it's all . . . Mr. Dennis' fault for pairing me up with him.

I thought trying to find someone to blame out of this mess, and at the moment Mr. Dennis appeared very blameworthy.

Finally the school day was over. I walked into my empty house, upstairs and up to my room to shower and change.

Once out of the bathroom and freshly clothed I made my way down to the kitchen to get something to eat. Snacks weren't what I was craving and I wasn't in the frame of mind for cooking so I picked up the phone and dialed the pizzeria closest to my house which happened to be like 25 minutes away and ordered.

As soon as I put down the phone the doorbell rang and I instantly dreaded going to answer it, but it was inevitable and so I walked to the foyer and opened the door to see none other than Ajay.

He was leaning against one of the columns looking just as sexy as he was dangerous. He leaned off and walked towards me. I stepped aside so he could stroll in. I closed the door and turned around to come face to face with him. I immediately backed away and walked past him into the kitchen. He followed and kept his distance which I was grateful for.

"Um, are you hungry?' I asked politely out of manners and for lack of anything else to say.

"Not right now," he said settling his eyes on me.

When I realized he wasn't going to say more I decided to speak so as to prevent an awkward silence.

"Well then let's start," I said pulling a notebook and pen out of the drawer on my right and placing it on the island between us.

"Here?" he asked arching his eyebrow.

I was confused as to what he meant. Where else would we go?

"Why not here?" I asked.

"Why not your room?" he replied with a hint of a smirk.

"My room's in a mess," I said the first thing that came to mind and it sounded like a good con until he said he didn't mind.

Then he reached for my wrist and led me out of the kitchen through the way we entered.

I couldn't help but notice the butterflies I felt in my stomach as his hand touched mine, but I waved it off.

What is wrong with you woman? Focus, he could be plotting your death!!

My better judgment screamed at me as he led me upstairs. At the top of the stairs he stopped and waited for me to show him which room was mine. I walked to the end of the hallway to the door that was closed all the while thinking of a way to get out of the situation. I reluctantly reached my hand forward and opened it and allowed him to go through first. He walked in and then turned around to me.

"Yeah, it's a real pig sty in here," his voice was laced with sarcasm.

"Well uh, the maid must have cleaned it," I lied. We didn't have a maid. But he didn't need to know that.

He arched his eyebrow and went over to my desk.

I shuffled cautiously over to my bed and sat on the edge, which depicted exactly how I was feeling.

"So where do you want to start?" I questioned as I watched him sitting in my chair as he assessed my room.

"Well I think I should get to know my partner a little more first," he said leaning back.

"Um, what do you want to know?" I asked timidly.

"Why so shy?" he asked with an amused voice. Still I don't seem to get what is so damned amusing.

"I'm always shy," I replied quickly.

He was quiet for a minute while he locked his eyes onto mine.

"Why have I never seen you around at school before?"

"Besides the fact that you're a senior and I'm a junior, I tend to be by myself and away from most people when not necessary," I answered

"What about Jamie?" he asked.

"What about her?" I asked wondering how he knew her, but then again, she used to be popular in that school. Everyone knows her.

He hesitated, forming his answer before he spoke, "You two seem to have become very close lately," he said shrugging like we were discussing the weather and not the affairs of my social life.

Why does it sound like he has been keeping a watchful eye on me?

Because he has, he's been practically stalking you!! And yet you are stupid enough to let him into your home without adult supervision.

"What if we have?" I asked.

"Do you always answer questions with questions?" he asked sounding amused.

"Maybe," I answered softly staring down at my hands folded neatly in my lap.

Silence pursued before he spoke once more.

"Do you have a boyfriend?" his casually stated words made me look up.

"How is that relevant?" I asked slightly embarrassed and confused as to why he asked that.

"It isn't, I'm just curious," he said with a mischievous glint in his eyes.

I chose to ignore that question as I opened my science text and flipped through the pages to the chapter the project was based on: Psychology; the scientific study of the human mind and mental states and of human and animal behavior.

"We could do a physical project, a written one, or both, using a human as lab rat as an example as to how our mind relates to certain actions or situations or we could-" I immediately stopped short as I noticed a pair of shoes in my peripheral vision. I looked up to come face to face with Ajay's neutral one a few inches too close to mine.

"So?" he asked.

I quickly shot up and backed away from him and my bed.

"So what?" I asked when I was a safe distance away.

He turned to face me his gorgeous green eyes locking onto mine.

"You didn't answer my question," he said walking over to me.

"I'd rather not."

"Why?" he asked still walking closer.

I decided to stand my ground not wanting a remake of what happened in school earlier today.

That whole trapped-with-your-back-against-the-wall was something to learn from.

"I choose not to," I said folding my arms across my chest.

He stopped in his tracks ending up a few feet away, still a safe distance.

"You've never had one, have you?" he asked looking slightly surprised and yet still amused.

This embarrassed me more than it should have. The fact that he knew;

not ever having a boyfriend wasn't something I was proud of when every other girl my age and even younger ones at our school had had at least two.

I didn't answer this time, looking down to stare abashedly at my feet.

Once again a pair of black converse made their way into my marginal vision causing me to look up.

"That's very hard to believe," he said smirking down at me.

I rolled my eyes and moved past him but his hand shot out and wrapped around my waist pulling my back into his chest. I let out a surprised yelp but my breath hitched in my throat as I suddenly felt his hot breath traveling across my neck and down my chest.

"Do you want one?" he asked.

Before I could stutter out an incoherent answer he had turned me around so that I was facing him. His arms around my waist had pulled me so close to him that I couldn't get my hands between us to push him away.

"No," I answered firmly trying to get loose of his tight grasp.

"Aw, why?" he asked staring me straight in the eyes.

I ignored his question, "Let me go."

"I don't want to, I'm kind of enjoying this, aren't you?" he asked dropping his hands to my hips and rubbing circles with his thumb on my exposed skin between my low rise jeans and my tank top, never once averting his eyes.

I tried pulling away which resulted in him pulling me closer to his body if that was even possible and lowering his lips to my collar bone. I was enjoying his attention, a little too much, I thought, letting out a soft sigh as his teeth teased my skin.

"Ajay," I said as firmly as I could manage and struggling yet again to get away from his hold.

"Mmm?" he asked soothing the spot with his tongue where his teeth had tortured a few moments before.

"Stop," I gasped out as I felt my self control weakening.

"Why?" he breathed huskily in my ear.

"Because I said so," I replied softly.

"You know you want it," he growled moving his lips over my heated skin.

And in reality I did want it; I loved the feel of his lips against my skin, his hands around me. I had never gotten attention like this from a male before and I was enjoying it, probably more than I should have. His lips trailed up my neck leaving butterfly kisses in their wake. He stopped and pulled away, his face centimeters from mine, his eyes mirroring my own.

He moved in slowly his lips a hairs distance from mine when we were both startled by the sound of the doorbell chiming throughout the otherwise silent house. His grip on me loosened and I took that as my opening to escape. I backed away quickly, color rising to my cheeks, my breathing uneven. I didn't look at him as I turned around quickly opened my door and ran downstairs to answer the front door.

I flung open the front door not in the least expecting to see the person on the other side of the threshold. A man about in his early twenties was holding a box of pizza in his hands and then I remembered I had ordered food before Ajay had shown up. I paid the man and thanked him, taking the pizza and closing the door. I walked to the kitchen placing the box on the countertop. I stood still for a moment letting my thoughts focus before I let out a troubled sigh.

How could I have been so stupid? I nearly kissed him and I don't even know him! I am so-

I was interrupted from my thoughts when the object of my frustration strolled into the room. I abruptly stiffened.

When he made no move to make me uncomfortable by placing himself in one of the bar stools I loosened up slightly.

"Um there's pizza, if you're hungry," I said unsure of myself gesturing to the box in front of him. He nodded while opening the box and taking a slice of pizza out and placing it in his mouth.

All the while he hadn't said anything and it was unnerving me. What was going through his head? What was he planning? His silence was making me nervous . . . how could he be so calm after what just took place?

Then I put two and two together. This was Ajay Edison I was dealing with, the boy was a chick magnet, and he had girls all over him. That was just something he did every day. It was nothing new to him. I was just something to pass the time. I felt my cheeks burning with embarrassment and shockingly disappointment as this thought came to mind. I brushed it off though, mentally scolding myself for believing anything other than what I stupidly had.

His voice made me jump.

"Aren't you hungry?" he asked gesturing to the pizza.

Now that he had mentioned it, the smell wafting throughout the kitchen was indeed making me hungry. I reached forward and took a slice for myself. I was about to take a bite when I felt his eyes on me. One thing I hated was people watching me while I ate. It made me feel more self conscious than I generally did. I nibbled a bit then put the slice on a napkin.

He raised a skeptical eyebrow at me but decided not to question as he continued eating.

"Full?" I asked as I realized he was leaning contentedly back in his chair, four slices from the box gone excluding the one I had taken.

"Yeah, for now," he said.

I took the box and placed it in the microwave for later as it was getting late and we hadn't even begun the project yet.

I was about to go back upstairs for the science text when I noticed it was sitting on the countertop alongside my notebook and my pen. He had brought it down which meant he was probably serious about starting the project now.

And I wasn't disappointed when an hour later we had finished writing the draft for the written part and had begun pooling our ideas for the physical sector of the project. Throughout that whole hour, not once did he make any advances towards me. I almost forgot what had taken place just an hour or so ago. If he decided to ignore what had happened then so would I.

At half past eight it was nearing darkness and I was expecting Ajay to go home soon so I closed the science text claiming I was tired. It might have had the desired effect I was hoping for if my stomach hadn't stubbornly intervened. It began to rumble right after I faked a yawn.

Ajay looked up from his place on the living room floor, across from me, and quirked an eyebrow.

"Maybe it's because you refuse to eat," he said in an accusing tone.

I didn't answer as I made my way towards the kitchen, Ajay in tow.

I poured myself a glass of orange juice and downed it to relive my stomach. I would have eaten something if he wasn't so intent on watching.

I put my glass in the sink deciding to wash it later. I turned to see Ajay watching me with a disapproving stare.

"What?" I asked.

"Why don't you eat something, there's still more pizza you know," he said walking over to the microwave and pulling out the box I placed in there earlier.

He shoved the box in my hands.

"I, um, I'll eat later," I said putting it back into his hands.

"You won't make it to later if you don't eat *now*," he said pushing it back into my grasp.

This was getting frustrating. I pushed it back to him.

There was a reason you never saw me in the cafeteria, it's because I don't like to eat in front of people dammit!

"I really don't understand why girls are anorexic, I mean most of them are already skinny as it is and then they think they are fat, it's stupid if you ask me," he said pushing the box right back into my hold.

Wait, what?

"You think I'm anorexic?" I asked incredulously almost dropping the box.

"Why else would you not want to eat when you're clearly hungry?' he asked skeptically.

Maybe its cause you're standing right there scrutinizing my every move!

"I don't feel comfortable eating around people," I admitted.

He furrowed his brows at me as if not believing my answer.

Why is he looking at me like that? Do I look anorexic to you? Yea, sure I may be thin, but that doesn't automatically mean I am anorexic. That's just being close minded and stereotypical.

I rolled my eyes in return.

"What?" I snapped.

"Why do you feel uncomfortable eating in front of people?" he asked.

What the hell kind of question is that? Why do birds fly? Cause they just do . . . jeez!

"I don't know, I just do," was the best response I could offer.

"Fine I won't look then, eat," he commanded gesturing to the pizza.

Why did he care if I ate or not? It was my choice. I forgot about that though as I took out a slice and heated it up in the microwave. I made sure he had turned around before I took my first bite. When I had taken my last bite I instructed him to turn back around.

"You are one of the weirdest girls I have ever encountered," he said turning around to face me with an amused grin.

I looked down in embarrassment.

"But I like that."

Ajay was confusing me more and more with each passing moment.

He went home a little after our food scenario, leaving me to eat all the pizza I wanted and to ponder the day's events.

November 16—Thursday

"And your partner is Dakota Richards," I finished telling Jamie of the project I had learned about the day before.

We were sitting under the bleachers during lunch time, she filling me in about her ultrasound and me telling her about the science project that had come up.

"Dakota's cute," she told me taking a bite out of her sandwich.

I nodded in agreement. He was the other school heartthrob beside Ajay and Tristan. I guess it's just fate that they were all best friends. The bad boys and hottest people in school.

As soon as the dismissal bell rang Jamie's mother had picked her up in the car park because of an important family matter that suddenly came up. Not having a reason to stay back in school I headed straight for the compound entrance as I left the building.

I pulled my i-pod out of my pocket and fumbled with the ear phones trying to untangle them from one another. As I was about to put them in my ear something landed on my shoulder making me jump and spin around.

"I figured we'd walk together since we're going the same place," Ajay said smiling as he fell in step beside me.

I stopped, making him turn to me with a skeptical expression.

"But I'm going home," I said confused.

"So am I," he said turning around to walk again.

"If I remember correctly your home was that way," I said pointing down the street in the opposite direction.

"I'm going to *your* home," he said as if it were the most obvious thing.

My eyes widened as reality suck in.

"But, I didn't invite you," I said bluntly before I could think of how rude that comment may have sounded.

"You don't need to, we have a project to do, I am going to be at your house a lot until we finish it," he said taking my hand and pulling me along with him in the direction of my house.

Well we had better finish it soon.

I opened the front door and we both ventured inside.

"We have to start on the actual paper we're going to give in since the draft is done, and then we need to think of an idea for the physical experiment, but we'll tackle that later, right now we need to start the paper," I said walking to the kitchen.

I turned around to face Ajay who was looking at me expectantly.

"What?" I asked.

"Let's go then," he said.

"Go where?" I asked confused. I thought he wanted to do the project at my house.

"To your room," he said it like it was the most obvious thing in the world.

What was with him and my room, the kitchen was perfectly fine in my eyes, it was bigger and had more escape routes if he were to try anything. Perfect location.

"Why, we can do it here," I challenged.

"But your room is much better," he said.

"Yeah, how?"

"It's more comfortable, and besides there's less chance of people walking in on us," he said shrugging.

"Here is just as comfy and so what if someone walks in, it's not as if we'd be doing anything bad," I replied not aware of the consequence of my words.

"We could be if you want," he said sending me a seductive smirk.

I rolled my eyes. He was way too sexually inclined, but then again he was an average teenage boy.

"Let's start," I said ignoring his comment.

I pulled out some paper and a pen when the idea struck me that we could print the assignment and it would be easier and faster than it being written. But then I also realized that there were no computers downstairs except for my mother's, in her room, which I never used.

"Wait right here, I'm gonna go get my laptop," I said as I put back the stuff I had just taken out and walked out of the kitchen.

I ran upstairs and grabbed my laptop out of its case and ran back downstairs and into the kitchen to see, surprisingly, that Ajay had stayed put. I motioned for him to follow me into the living room where I set up on the mahogany desk.

For the rest of the hour Ajay and I worked on the assignment; editing and adding pieces where we thought necessary. Halfway through typing it out the screen's page froze. I tapped a few keys but nothing happened. I sighed in frustration and glared at the screen. This had never happened before so I had no idea of what to do next.

Ajay, who had been sitting next to me tossing a paperweight back and forth, looked over and sighed as he saw the predicament I was in. He got up and stood behind my chair and before I knew what he was doing I felt his hot breath fanning the side of my neck and his arms had come around me as he brushed my hands from the keyboard. My breath caught in my throat as he started typing away. Keeping my eyes fixed firmly on the screen, not having anywhere better to put them, I saw that the page had unstuck. I expected him to move since he had fixed the problem so I was surprised when he continued typing. My heart sped up a little more as I was aware that our position was being prolonged. Then my eyes scanned the words appearing on the screen.

I've got an idea for the experiment. We can show them how your mind and body reacts whenever I get close to you. How hot and bothered you get. Like when I do this . . .

Before I could register what the end of the note suggested I felt soft, moist lips come in contact with my skin. I couldn't move my hands to push him away because they were soon captured by his own as he laced his fingers with mine. I felt so weak, my knees would have given away if I weren't sitting. I was fighting and loosing an internal battle. In a weak attempt to get away from his lips I pulled my head away, turning it to the side, which only resulted in giving him more access, which he willingly accepted, sucking on the alcove of my neck and collar bone which so happens to be my sweet spot. I couldn't help it. A soft moan escaped my lips as I gave up trying to fight him.

His hands slid from mine and traced their way up my arms slowly. He continued kissing my neck as his hands made their way to my shoulders. He slid my strap over my shoulder. Somehow in my state of helpless bliss I knew I didn't want him to go that far, in fact I wasn't even so sure that I wanted him to start in the first place, but before I could stop him someone else did me the favor.

"Brooklynn, take your boyfriend and go to your room, I have guests coming over in a few minutes," an annoyed voice startled me and I am pretty sure it startled Ajay too when I saw his shocked expression, though it didn't last for long.

We pulled apart, me with a guilty face and Ajay with a neutral one, to face my mother standing in the entrance foyer with her designer outfit and matching suitcase resting behind her.

Well it looks like she came back from her business trip. I was never informed when she was leaving or arriving from a business trip unless I asked so I wasn't expecting to have my mother walking in on us.

I stood up quickly and closed my laptop and walked out of the living room to the stairwell. I expected Ajay to follow me, which he did after briefly declaring his name to my mother.

I walked into my room waiting for Ajay to come in. When he did I slammed the door behind him. I was suddenly angry and frustrated with him as well as myself.

I whipped around to glare at him lying contentedly on my bed.

"What is with you?" I half whispered half yelled at him striding over to rest my laptop down.

"What do you mean?" he asked innocently.

I suddenly wanted to climb onto that bed and wrap my hands around his neck, but that image soon morphed into something totally different and I had to shake myself for thinking such things.

Stay focused woman, you are angry right now, I scolded myself mentally.

As I looked at him I forgot what I was going to say next so I just settled for glaring at him. He only smirked in return which made me groan in frustration. I turned my back to him, going to my desk and flipping open my laptop to continue the paper I was typing. The screen lit up after a moment and went back to Microsoft Word. I blushed as I glanced at the screen where Ajay had last typed. I hastily deleted it though, continuing the paper while still ignoring the gorgeous pain on my bed.

I was deep in thought five minutes later contemplating whether or not I should leave out a not so necessary paragraph, but I decided against it as I figured it would make the paper longer anyway and content was key as Mr. Dennis had put it.

"Is your mom always like that?" his voice interrupted the silence.

I didn't bother to turn or look at him.

"Yes," I answered not pausing in my fast typing.

After a few moments of silence he broke it again.

"Why?" he asked.

"She just is," I answered beginning to glare at the screen.

It was easy when I told Jamie the whole deal with my mother and I, but there was no way I was divulging that to him. Jamie wasn't one to question; she just nodded in understanding when I told her which I was thoroughly grateful for. Ajay, I wasn't so sure what his reaction would be and I was far from trusting him anyway.

He remained quiet after that as he must have figured I didn't want to go into the topic of my supercilious mother. You can't blame me for not being fond of the idea that I was an unwanted child.

Ten minutes of silence later the doorbell rang. Ajay looked up from his spot on the bed to watch me expectantly.

"What?" I asked in mid type.

"Those are your mom's guests, right?" he asked looking at me.

"I guess so," I answered not really caring one way or the other.

"Well it's impolite to not introduce yourself, isn't it?" he asked turning over to lie on his stomach.

"I thought she made it clear that she didn't want me there, don't you think?" I asked sarcastically.

"Your mom's a bitch," he said more to himself than me.

It took me by surprise, I didn't feel offended in the least, but I was surprised, I didn't think he felt so free to express himself. I actually appreciated it.

"At least we agree on something," I muttered going back to typing.

Yet he had heard me and sat up.

"That can't be true, I'm sure there are many other things we agree on," he said.

"Like?" I asked half paying attention to him while I scanned the screen for errors.

"Let's see . . . what's your favorite color?" he asked.

Yeah, that's original.

"I don't have one."

"How could you not have a favorite color?" he asked as if it were weird not to like one specific color out of endless.

"Well do you have one, then?" I asked turning the question on him.

"Yes, pink," he said without hesitation.

Once again I stopped typing to look at him. I quirked an eyebrow in disbelief.

"Pink?" I asked doubting he was telling the truth.

"Yes, is there a problem with that?" he asked crossing his hands over his chest in defense.

I scanned his face to see if he was kidding, so finding no hint of a smile I answered.

"No, not in the least," I hesitated before adding, "I just find it unusual for someone like you to like . . . pink."

"Someone like me . . . what's that supposed to mean?"

"You just don't seem like a pink kind of guy, you don't have the traits, no offense" I said.

"None taken, and what traits do I need to be a '"pink' guy?" he asked raising his hands and making the air quotations for the word pink.

I thought about it before I began counting a few qualities off my fingers, "Compassion, lovingness, charm, sensitivity, romantic-" he cut me off.

"Who ever said I don't have those traits?" he asked getting defensive.

"Well you never show them so how is anyone supposed to know?"

"Just because you haven't seen them doesn't mean I don't have them."

"Right, so you're telling me when you're not being the school's bad boy, you're off saving kittens in trees," I said sarcastically.

"I have all those qualities," he said.

"Really?" I asked.

"I can be compassionate, loving, charming, sensitive, and—" I cut him off.

"To your dog maybe, but to people, I have my doubts."

"And romantic," he finished ignoring my interruption.

I spun around in my chair to fully face him.

"Romantic? Don't make me laugh!" I snorted.

"I can be very romantic," he countered.

"Really? What have you ever done for a girl that's considered romantic?" I challenged.

He seemed to think for a moment until his eyes brightened and he replied.

"Perfect example, a few minutes ago," he answered smirking.

I had to rewind for a moment to register what he was talking about.

"That? You call that romantic? Please Ajay, that was sexual assault," I scoffed.

It was his turn to look at me in disbelief.

"Assault? Are you kidding me? You enjoyed that more than anything," he said sliding a customary smirk into place.

"Did not," I retorted.

"Yes you did, I heard you moaning in my ear," he said smugly.

"I didn't moan. I . . . sighed."

"In pleasure," he added.

"In frustration," I shot back.

He rolled his eyes and sat down on my bed.

"We both know that you liked it," he said.

"Did not," I muttered turning back to the screen.

"Whatever you say, we both know the truth so I guess we can call it our . . . dirty little secret," he whispered the last part loud enough for me to hear and sexily enough for it to send shivers up my spine.

Damn him!

I finished typing out our report and sat back relaxing my overworked fingers. I couldn't truly protest because Ajay did facilitate, he had, after all, written the draft which was, in all fairness to him, much harder than typing.

"It's finished?' he asked looking up from playing around with one of my many throw pillows.

"Finally," I answered.

"Now what?" he asked.

I turned to him.

"What do you mean '*now what*'?"

"What are we supposed to do now, now that the report is done? I mean you can't expect us to start on the experiment," he stated.

That's true, I was tired and wasn't up for starting the second part of the assignment today. That was asking for too much.

"Uh, I don't know," I said shaking my head slightly.

"I'm hungry," he said right before his stomach growled in alliance.

So was I, but my mother's guests hadn't left yet, their cars were still in our driveway.

"The guests are still here," I said.

"So . . . wait, you mean your mother won't even let you come down even if you're hungry," he asked clearly shocked.

I stared at him brazenly which brought across my point. He hesitated as if to think, then he pulled my hand forcing me to get up and led me across my room.

"What are you doing?" I asked pulling my hand from his grasp making him turn around.

"Well I'm hungry and I want something to eat, if we can't go downstairs we'll just sneak out and get dinner elsewhere," he said like it was the perfect solution.

I, on the other hand found so many flaws with that plan though.

"You can't be serious, what are you going to do, jump out the window?" I asked sarcastically.

"Exactly," he said walking towards the window that faced the neighbor's house.

Hello, sarcasm, I was kidding!

"My room is on the second floor," I said hoping that would knock some sense into him.

"You mean to tell me you have never sneaked out before?" he asked turning to me, not the response I was aiming for.

An 'Oh you're right how stupid of me to think that we could actually make it,' would have met my terms just fine.

"Of course I've never snuck out, I have no reason to," I replied.

"Well now you do," he said pulling open my window and getting up on the ledge.

Before I could tell him to stop, like he'd listen, he dropped from my sight. I let out a twisted sound between a gasp and a shriek and ran to my window looking down frantically to see if I spotted the mangled form of Ajay Edison on my front lawn. I was more than relieved and even bewildered when I saw a perfectly fine Ajay standing at the base of my window dusting himself off.

"Obviously you've done this before," I said not too loud afraid that I might draw attention to us from the people downstairs.

He just smirked and looked expectantly up at me.

Was he waiting for me to jump? He must be delusional.

"What are you waiting for?" he called up in a hushed tone.

"I'd rather not break my neck trying to jump out of a second storied window," I hissed at him.

"You won't break your neck, I'll catch you, don't worry," he replied.

Don't worry? He must be kidding me.

I shook my head firmly.

"Just jump. Aren't you hungry?" he asked.

Shit. I was definitely hungry, there was no denying that, but what's a little hunger for a possibly broken neck? I looked down at Ajay's reassuring expression. I wanted to jump, I mean I had never done anything exciting before since I never had the chance and I wanted some action. This was opportunity knocking on my door and I had better take it.

So with that in mind I made a grab for money in my bedside table shoving it in my pocket and stepped cautiously onto the ledge of my window. I looked down to see Ajay with his arms ready to catch me. I closed my eyes took a deep breath and leapt, praying to God that he would catch me.

When I didn't feel any pain of breaking bones and the rush of air around me had stopped I deemed it safe to open my eyes. The first thing I saw were gorgeous green ones staring down at me. I looked around and noticed that I was safely off the ground in Ajay's arms. How he managed to catch a 120 pound girl falling from two floors up is beyond me, I know he was toned and had more than average muscles, but still.

"Afraid I would drop you?" he asked never losing his smirk.

"Yes," I replied bluntly.

Of course I was afraid.

He set me down and I fixed my shirt.

"Where to?" I asked.

"Where do you want to go?" he questioned.

"Ok, let's go to Spinner's" I decided, then we headed in the direction of the well known 60's restaurant a few blocks down from my house.

He agreed, falling in step with me on our way.

I was wondering if he liked onion rings, because that's what Spinner's specialized in . . . then I realized while he knew at least a little about me I only knew his favorite color was pink

"Do you have any siblings?" I asked out of the blue, well it appeared that way since I broke the silence between us.

He turned to me with a quirked eyebrow.

"No, I'm an only child," he answered though. I believed it safe to continue.

"How old are you?" I asked the first thing that popped into my mind. I had to be in his presence a lot more beyond today and I had no idea of how old he might be.

"18," he answered staring straight ahead without missing a beat.

We reached the little restaurant in record time. A waiter showed us to a booth near a window where Ajay and I sat opposite each other.

After our orders were made I noticed that neither one of us had made a move to strike up a conversation. I was fine with that since I still felt a little uneasy around him. I'm not going to lie to you, I feared him. Not a whole lot, but it was evident and it was there. He intimidated me and I am pretty sure he knew it too. He just had the words 'rebel, badass, dangerous,' seething from his stance. But I had no choice but to put up with him, he was my partner for the project we had yet to finish.

Once again I found myself scolding Mr. Dennis' lack of proper decision-making in my head, I mean what right did he have to pair me up with someone like Ajay? I was Brooklynn Vladimir, no one really knew who I was, I was the quiet girl who sat at the back of the class steering her way out of attention, just an above average student who minded her own business and suddenly Mr. Dennis catches a lapse in mental capacity and decides to pair me up with the total opposite.

No matter how civil I acted towards Ajay I still held a sense of apprehension in my mind. He was the school's playboy, the last title I wanted to associate myself with and I let my morals down by letting him practically ravage me twice in my own home. And I had done nothing to stop him. I was weak, too weak and I need to have strength if I were dealing with Ajay.

Conversation was at a minimum as we ate our meals. Ajay didn't give the impression that he was willing to chat but he didn't make any attempts to back out of any conversation either. So it was mostly me asking him questions about himself and him answering with precise and to the point replies.

I don't think he noticed, but the waitress that served us was a little too interested in his order for it to be considered professional hospitality. The obvious way she batted her eyelashes and lingered just a few moments longer than was necessary, even the way she leant over the table to reveal her breasts were apparently oblivious to Ajay. It's like it didn't bother him in the least that the chick was brazenly checking him out.

He didn't pay any more attention to her than was necessary, which left me slightly confused. I had been engaging him in conversation and even though it was obvious he'd rather not be a part of it, he humored me anyway.

I didn't dwell too long on the fact though as we continued to eat our meals in peace. We paid for our food and left the restaurant. Upon leaving the building I glanced up to the sky and it was obvious that nightfall was nearing. I cursed in my mind.

Crap, it's almost eight . . .

For a reason unbeknown to me, I was never comfortable with reaching home after my mother.

The walk was silent. Neither one of us had spoken since we entered the diner. We made it back to my house in five minutes or so and then it hit me that the only way to get inside was to use the door. You see, my window was up on the second floor and beneath its sill it only had the flat surface of the brick wall all the way to the ground, no trellis, which meant, it was only a one way route.

Clenching my jaw in frustration I berated myself for not thinking of that when I thoughtlessly leapt from my window.

I knew if I were to open the door and walk in, my mother wouldn't really care so I blew off my frustration and walked up the pebbled pathway to the door. Besides, her guests were still over because the five or so expensive cars parked in our drive way were dead giveaways. I opened the door to be greeted by soft laughs and the clinking of glasses. I walked into the foyer and with Ajay following and realized that I could easily make my way upstairs without being recognized since no one was in the living room to spot us, and besides they would be too tipsy anyway to care. I knew my mother's get-togethers well enough to know the outcome of most and by the slurred words coming from the kitchen, this was no exception.

I rolled my eyes lightly and softly padded up the stairs. I entered my room making sure to lock the door after we were in to prevent and wandering guests from entering which earned a perked eyebrow look from Ajay.

I slightly tilted my head, whatever perverted thoughts he had running through his head I put a stop to, "Please, there are half drunk men downstairs," I said gliding past him to drop tiredly on my bed.

He turned around to face me, "You really think they'd come up here, with your mother right downstairs?" he asked skeptically.

If he only knew . . .

"It's happened before," I said stating my point.

His eyes widened if only slightly.

"What does your mother do?"

"What is she supposed to do?" I asked cynically.

He sensed my bitterness and answered.

"If I ever had a daughter I would never let a guy within reach of her, all men are bastards, who only want one thing" he said firmly.

Yourself included . . .

"How is that fair? You can't keep her away from guys forever you know," I said looking at him.

"I can try."

"She'd hate you," I countered.

"I don't care, I wouldn't want my daughter chased by sex crazed men," he answered.

I didn't bother to answer the many retorts I had snapping in my mind, instead I asked, "What time do you plan on leaving?"

He didn't seem to be put off by my bluntness; he only shrugged as he answered.

"I don't know, I'd be bored if I went home, so I think I'll crash here," he said sitting on my bed at my feet.

It took me a moment to register his answer. I sat up and flared at him. "You can't" I said.

"Why not?" he asked.

What do you mean "why not?" I said you can't, I don't want you to sleeping over at my house! I don't even know you!

"First of all, we hardly know each other, second, it'd be inappropriate-" before I could get started on the third reason he cut me off.

"That's not true, we do know each other, or we could while I am here, and how is it inappropriate? It's not like I am a complete stranger or a drunken guy who would try to rape you," he said pointedly which made me remember my mother's friends downstairs.

A voice suddenly materialized in my mind.

Let him stay . . .

What, no, I can't let him stay!

Why not?

Because . . .

Yeah, that explains it.

Shut up, he is not sleeping over.

See, this is why you have no friends, you're so lame, let him stay!

Sigh but-

No buts just let him spend the night, maybe it'll turn out for the best and you might become friends by morning.

I highly doubt it.

Stop being a stick in the mud and let him stay.

. . . well . . . fine.

I can't believe I just fought an internal battle in my head and lost!

"Fine," I said.

"What?" he asked confused.

"You can stay," I said softly not liking the fact that I was giving in to my audacious subconscious, although it seemed to be more of an alter ego.

"Alright, thanks," he said falling back onto my bed.

I watched him expectantly for a few moments until he looked up at me, "What?" he asked.

"Don't you want to call home and tell someone you're spending the night?" I asked.

"Nope, parents aren't home," he said putting his hands behind his head while looking up at me.

"Okay then."

An hour later and the guests were still here, I was still annoyed at myself for letting him spend the night, though we had settled into a casual talk having never left my bed.

We had begun to play a game of 'this or that' after agreeing that we in fact hardly knew each other.

"Moon or stars?" I asked.

"Moon."

"Skittles or chocolate?"

"Skittles," I answered, chocolate wasn't really a favorite of mine anyway, "cookies or milk?"

"Cookies and cream," he answered.

A combo. And my favorite flavor of ice cream

The game continued and I figured Ajay to have a few similarities with me which surprised me a whole lot because if I hadn't heard it from him I would have never guessed half of those things were true. Halfway through the game his bladder got the better of him and he excused himself to use the bathroom. While he was absent from the room my mind began to wander.

I cannot believe we are actually getting along . . .

Why is that so hard to believe, he's not as bad as you make him out to be

Well that's true, but still, look at his reputation, he is no doubt a bad influence

So what, he's defied the law a few times, doesn't mean he's a terrible person . . .

Whatever, at least you're giving him a chance, I'm proud of you

Sigh yea, I guess you're right

Guess? Please, I am always right

Don't push it

Ok, ok . . .

At that moment Ajay walked back into the room, and I had no choice but to stop the mental conversation between myself and my alter ego. Whoa, I must be going mad; talking to yourself is always the first sign of insanity.

He walked over and stationed himself in the same spot he had been in before he had left sitting crossed legged on my bed opposite of me, who was in the same position.

We took no hesitation in continuing the game where we had left off.

During the game I found myself loosening up just a bit towards him which led to some of the bold questions I had asked him, one being

"Make out with Tristan or Dakota?"

His face broke out into a smile, which was not what I was expecting, before he answered.

"Both, they're both first-rate kissers." I nearly choked on the air I was breathing. Did I just hear that properly? I coughed a bit before I looked up to see his smirking face.

"You've already made out with them?" I asked.

He nodded seemingly amused by my reaction.

"Why?" was the only question that seemed smart to ask at the moment.

"We were at this party and some of the girls sort of ganged up on us and made us do it, at first we weren't sure, but we did it and it wasn't so bad," he shrugged as if this was nothing.

I still had a hard time figuring out why the girls would want them to do that, an even harder time concluding why they had agreed to it and yet the hardest time believing that Ajay would do something like that. But then again I was learning new things about him that I never thought of by just looking at him, which I had always done. That term 'never judge a book by its cover' was beginning to make light in this situation.

"Were they drunk when they asked you?" I asked.

"No, it turns them on, to see guys making out," he explained like it was the weather he was talking about and I was starting to feel like a little kid learning things for the first time. So sue me, I wasn't experienced in any of this.

"It does?"

"So you mean you've never seen two guys kissing before?" he asked like I was supposed to.

I shook my head, no.

"I'll just have to show you what it looks like, remind me later," he said.

"Okay?" I said uncertain that I wanted to see it anyway.

"It's pretty much the same as guys being turned on by girls making out," he said.

I scrunched up my face in disgust a little, "Yeah, I still don't see what's so hot about that."

"When you see two guys at it, then you'll tell me otherwise," he replied.

"I beg to differ," I muttered not believing that I would ever be turned on by that.

Little did I know . . .

Once again in the middle of the game Ajay had to excuse himself to go to the bathroom, it was undoubtedly the result of having three glasses of soda at Spinner's for dinner. I just hoped that his sugar intake tolerance was high because I wasn't sure I was ready for an overly hyper Ajay yet, but I am pretty sure I don't have to worry about that. I had taken to staring at the ceiling in the first few moments after his departure. How was it that I had never known that my ceiling had an in-depth design engraved into the plaster? You'd think that after spending countless nights in my bed I would have at least looked up once to stare at the intricate design of my ceiling, but apparently that was not the case.

I began tracing the engravings with my eyes and became so caught up that I didn't bother to look at Ajay when he came through the door. Only when I felt the bed depress I looked down. My eyes widened and my face paled considerably as I realized that the fully intoxicated man a few feet across from me was not Ajay Edison.

I scrambled off of the bed nearly falling to the floor in the process. I regained my balance and backed away. The man looked up at me with unfocused eyes.

"Aw, sweets, where are you going?" he asked with slightly slurred speech.

"Get out!" I tried to say firmly, but my voice was shaking in fear.

"That isn't any way to talk to a guest," he replied standing shakily and took a step forward.

"Get out," I repeated loosing the little courage I had.

He took a few more wobbly steps forward making me more frightened than before. I was so scared I didn't think about moving so instead of taking a step back my feet were planted to the same spot on the floor.

"Don't be like that, love, don't you remember what happened the last time?" he asked now so close I could smell the stench of alcohol on his breath. My eyes burned from the sting of his breath mixing with the tears that pooled as a memory flashed before my eyes.

He leaned down even closer grabbing roughly onto my arm and pulling me closer to him as I tried to pull away to no avail. He wasted no time in bringing his face closer to mine, I shut my eyes waiting for the worst and not at all expecting to hear the deep voice of my savior.

"What the hell?!" an angry voice reached my frightened ears.

My arm was suddenly released, I backed away rubbing the already forming bruise where his fingers had dug into my skin. A sickening crack resonated around the room and forced me to look up. The intoxicated man was staggering backwards holding his now bloody nose and Ajay was seething with anger as he advanced on the guy again.

"You sick bastard," he muttered as he socked the still staggering man a punch in the face.

I just stood there in shock and a revived fear of watching Ajay beat a man nearly twice his age. He looked angry, very angry, no doubt there, and it was slightly unnerving. I had heard way too many rumors, enough to know that when Ajay was angry that was when he was at his worst. And his worst was scary. I found myself backing into the far corner of my room away from the two of them.

He was about to advance on the man again when a totally involuntary gasp escaped my lips. He paused before whispering to the guy in a dangerously low tone, "Get the f**k out!"

Maybe it was the fact that he had just received a fine beating or he wasn't as stupid as I thought, but the man quickly wobbled his way out of the room holding his bloodied face.

Oh sure, when I tell him to get out he ignores my commands, but when Ajay does it he's ready to obey. Ok sure, he throws in a beating and a profanity or two, but still . . .

Anyway, back to the problem at hand. I looked up at Ajay to see him breathing heavily with his knuckles clenched at his side. His eyes still held the same vicious fury, but as he looked at me a tingle of regret flashed across them momentarily. I think it was my expression, which was somewhere between complete fright and wariness.

He took a cautious step towards me to which I shrunk back into the wall as much as I could. He stepped back immediately, mumbled a soft "sorry", turned and walked out of the room.

A few seconds later I was still against the wall when that annoying voice decided to grace me with its figment presence.

What is wrong with you?

Me?!

Yes you! He just saved you from a potential rape scene and all you do is treat him like he was the one who tried to rape you?

He just kicked a guy's ass that was twice his age!

So, he works out, big whoop. He just saved you and he's the one to end up saying sorry!

I sighed as I realized that was true, he had in fact just saved me and when he saw my reaction *he* ended up *apologizing*. He had no need to apologize, I didn't even thank him. Maybe I was being a bit too harsh to have reacted to him like that, but I couldn't help but think what would have gone down if I hadn't gasped. Would he have done more harm or worse yet killed him? I had seen his eyes; they were filled with pure rage and blinding fury, the kind that keeps you from acting rationally. That still scared me about him, but looking at the fact that he had done that for me made me more fond and appreciative of him weather I wanted to be or not.

Maybe I should apologize for the way I acted

Maybe?

Fine.

I sighed inwardly as I pushed away from the comforts of my corner and cautiously made my way out of my room. I turned the way I had seen Ajay turn and continued down the hallway. I peered into each of the rooms as I passed by, on the third door I figured it was obvious which room he was in by the light I had seen through the crack under the door of one of the few guest rooms.

I pushed open the door slightly to see him lying on the bed. I opened the door a little more and slipped through, closing it behind me. I silently took a breath and walked over to the bed where I sat at the edge of it. His eyes were staring intently at one spot on the ceiling though I was pretty sure he wasn't really seeing it, due to the dazed look in them.

"I'm sorry, and thank you," I said calmly looking down at my hands. Apologizing wasn't something I liked doing or had much or any experience in so sue me if it wasn't a heart wrenching speech like in all the movies.

I wasn't sure if I was expecting a response or not, but when I didn't get one I decided that that was my cue to leave. I went to stand up and walk out the room, but his voice made me stop.

"Why are you sorry?" he asked softly.

I turned around and looked at him laying peacefully on the bed, but his eyes, the peace didn't reside there, and his eyes were troubled and pained like he was enduring some sort of torture.

I went back to the bed and took my spot next to him.

"For being such a bitch," I said.

"You weren't a bitch," he assured me, but I still thought otherwise.

"I shouldn't have acted that way," I said.

"Neither should I" he replied.

I had no reply to that one so I just lay there silently, before I told him thank you again.

Instead of the traditional 'You're welcome' I got, "You were serious when you said that's happened before?"

"Why would I lie about something like that?" I asked.

"Has it happened often?" he asked.

I didn't like where this conversation was going.

I tried to brush aside the topic; I think he caught on because he just asked again, "Has it?"

"Not really," I lied.

He stared at me intensely as silence prolonged itself between us. I shifted my gaze because it felt as though he could tell I was lying. I wasn't an exceptional liar, but I didn't suck, like other people. I heard him sigh, when I looked up his eyes were back to staring at one certain spot straight off into space.

I lost track of time after the first few minutes of just sitting there aimlessly beside him while he gazed off into space, I didn't bother saying anything because he looked so peacefully deep in thought. I was beginning to feel drowsy when his voice broke through the silence.

"Come on."

I looked over to see him getting off the bed. I looked up to him questioningly.

"You have school tomorrow, you should get some sleep," he said waiting for me to get up also, which I did.

I had gotten changed for bed modestly when he wasn't in the room. It had been arranged that he would sleep in the guest room for the night . . . what you thought I would let him sleep in my room? Ha!

I locked my door making sure no more replays of tonight would happen. As I turned over in my bed to get comfortable under the duvet, I thought about Ajay. What were my feelings towards him? At first I'd be intimidated, then I'd hate his guts, then I would get all friendly, then right back to the intimidation. It was like a cycle. It was hard not to like him and then it was easy not to as well. Does that even make any sense?

What did I consider him? A friend? An enemy? But then a person would not let an enemy sleep over. A friend wouldn't sexually harass a friend either. So what the hell was he? I don't know. I guess we were . . . acquaintances?

With that thought in mind I drifted off to sleep.

November 17—Friday

Beep—Beep—Beep—Beep B—

My hand flew out and slapped away the annoying contraption away from me. Sadly it didn't hit the wall and shatter into a million tiny pieces like I had imagined, but merely fell to the floor. The maddening beeping continued until I reached a sleepy hand to the back of my night table and pulled out the cord. I snuggled back unto my pillow. Beep—beep—beep. What the hell? I looked from my pillow to see the bright red numbers glaring at me from the floor and the incessant noise still continued. I rolled off my bed and landed right next to the agitating clock.

"How are you still alive?" I asked it stupidly, then I remembered that it worked with backup batteries.

What was I thinking when I decided it would be a good idea to have a battery operated alarm clock is beyond me.

I hit the snooze button, which I realized I should have just done in the first place. Then my phone's alarm followed. I flipped it open to shut it off and made my still sleepy way to my bathroom.

Minutes later I was tying the laces to my blue and white Airwalk when there was a knock at my door.

I stood confused as to what my mother would want and opened the door. My eyes widened a little as I saw Ajay.

Oh right, he slept over last night, it wasn't a dream.

I covered up my surprise quickly, but then the confusion as to why he was only wearing a bathrobe set in.

"Um, can I help you?" I asked.

He pushed past me and walked into my room.

"Yes you can," he said walking towards my drawer and opening the first draw.

"Excuse me, that's my stuff you're going through," I said coming up beside him to close my draw filled with all my t shirts.

He pulled out a few t shirts before I could close the draw.

"School starts in half hour and I don't have time to go home and get clothes," he said throwing a green t shirt over his head that said 'I'm a stupid genius' on the front.

He grabbed a pair of one of my hardly used skinny jeans since it was a size too big—which defeated the purpose of it being skinny—from the second drawer and wriggled into it.

The end product was no different from how he usually dressed, which made me ask, "Do you shop in the girls department or something?"

"Sometimes," he answered like there was nothing wrong with that.

I just sat back as he turned to the mirror and teased his hair into the normal style he wore to school.

"Your mom isn't here," he said looking at me in the mirror as he applied some (my) eyeliner to his gorgeous eyes.

"She leaves for work early sometimes," I answered.

He just nodded as he finished applying the eyeliner.

I looked down at my watch to notice that we only had ten minutes until the bell rang.

"We need to leave now," I said shortly before I walked out of my room and down to the kitchen.

I grabbed an apple and tossed it into my bag. I filled a glass of apple juice and downed it right before Ajay walked into the kitchen looking like he was ready for a fashion show and not just school.

I waited while he got a glass of milk to drink then I walked out the door with him in tow. I looked again at my watch and saw that we had eight minutes to get to school.

"Chill, we'll make it," he said smoothly from beside me. I sighed in return and kept up my hurried pace which he had no trouble keeping up with due to the fact that he was taller than me and hand longer legs.

Like last night at dinner, talk was scarce between us. But we did manage to get one thing out of the way.

"We'll talk about the rest of the project later," he briefed me soon before we arrived.

I nodded having no verbal response ready and kept walking alongside him still with the uncertainty of what our relationship could be considered as because at this rate I doubt we were much of friends.

As we reached the school gates we still had two minutes till the bell rang for the beginning of the day. Luckily for me or for him (I hadn't decided yet) there was no one around to witness our arrival at school together. Everyone was most definitely in the halls trying not to be late for class.

I didn't even bother to bid him goodbye as we separated to our different class a few lucky seconds before the bell rang.

Not like he expects one anyway.

Third period let out and I made my way to the official rendezvous for me and Jamie. And as expected she was already sitting there eating an assortment of fruits.

I walked over and sat down next to her.

"You came!" she exclaimed.

I gave her an odd look then remembered I wasn't early this morning as usual and she only sees me at lunch time.

"Yeah, I got held back this morning," I vaguely answered, returning her side hug.

"Want some?" she asked gesturing to the bowl of fruits she was munching on.

I kindly denied her offer pulling my own apple from my bag. I didn't want to deprive her. The reason she brought fruits to school today as well as every other day for the past week was because the doctor told her she should eat healthily so her mother, being excited about the pregnancy took the gesture to heart and has her on a strict diet of only healthy foods.

And if she is ever to forget that whenever she gets a craving for junk food or candy, it's her mother's and my job to remind her that it was all for the good of the baby.

Jamie and I sat and chatted for the rest of the lunch break about things (life) in general. Topics evolved and we found ourselves discussing the situation with her uninformed ex (whose identity I had yet to discover).

"When are you planning on telling him?" I asked.

"I don't know."

"Why don't you want to tell him again?"

"Well, I don't think he'd take it well, or want responsibility for it."

"Don't you think it's only fair that he knows that he is bringing a child into this world?"

"Well . . . yea, but it would be just easier if I prolonged the part where I tell him."

In my mind the longer she took the harder it would become, but who was I to judge?

I sighed as I realized that Jamie wasn't ready to inform her ex that he had gotten her pregnant so I switched topics.

"So, how's the project going with Dakota?" I asked.

"It's better than I expected, did I ever mention to you that he is adorable?" she asked.

Hmm, that's a first. On the norm she would call a guy hot or something, but never . . . adorable, he must be different then . . . hmm, especially with the way she's trying to suppress that smile

"Oh, you're blushing," I teased.

"Am not," she denied knowing I was right.

"So, what did you do?" I asked attention sparked.

"Nothing much, but there was this moment where we were both reaching for something and he sort of grabbed my wrist thinking it was it, cause he wasn't watching," she explained to me with an ever present smile adorning her features.

Ooh looks like someone's got a crush.

You're one to talk . . .

What do you mean?

Cough Ajay cough . . .

Shut up

You know it's true.

. . .

I pushed aside the annoying voice and focused on the babbling about Dakota.

The day couldn't finish fast enough. I walked home in a quicker pace than usual, eager to retire to my haven. I hadn't been there in a few days due to the hectic project for science as well as the recent heavy rains and I think this break was needed.

I sighed heavily as I sat silently relishing in the breeze sweeping the hair off my face and shoulders and calming my being instantly. My detached gaze focused in on the screen as music from the webpage started playing.

My entire evening was spent well at my station under my favorite oak tree in that deserted private field. My mind was void of all the events occurring lately in my life and I was perfectly fine with the lack of focus in that area.

Upon reaching home, my mother was still absent, no worries though. I silently made my way upstairs and into my room where I replaced my laptop where it is usually found, on my desk charging . . .

Some time, lying aimlessly on my bed, absent mindedly flipping through endless channels, my mind began to drift. I had been through two days with Ajay and I wasn't completely sure yet if the end result could be considered as good or bad. It was confusing enough as it was so my mind deliberately shifted to something less problematic.

Jamie and her web of social incidents. She was at the ripe age of sixteen, yet having all her previous friends abandon her because of her unexpected pregnancy with her ex whom she's too fearful to inform.

As I pondered this I realized I still had yet to learn of this ex-boyfriend of hers. I was beginning to think it was a guy who went to a different school, or lived in a different state or something. Although it wasn't my business if she didn't want to tell me, but I couldn't help but feel curious as to whom the hidden identity belonged to

I was still contemptuous of the idea that she waited to tell the guy of his conceived child. He had every right to know that he was bringing a child into this world no matter how his reaction may have been. No matter who he was, it was only fair . . .

And these thoughts were the last to grace my mind as I drifted off into sleep.

November 18—Saturday

The silence answered the unasked question of my mother's absence. Another lonely day. I sat up and swung my feet to the side of my bed as I rubbed the sleep out of my eyes.

Once I could see clearly I glanced around at my room. The walls painted a light blue, void of any posters—they disrupt the calm vibe that the blue walls emitted—and everything neatly stacked in its place.

I let out an annoyed sigh. This was what I went to sleep with and woke up to everyday and quite frankly it was beginning to get a little too monotonous for me. Why was it that my life eluded any sense of adventure? I was in the prime of my adolescence and the most action I got was avidly surfing the net and or talking to cyber strangers whose only replies consisted of incessantly overused abbreviations such as 'lol' and overrated emoticons to represent emotions.

I rolled my eyes at nothing in particular and got off my bed.

Downstairs, the silence seemed to have lifted due to the hum of the kitchen appliances and the occasional car passing down the road outside.

The glass of orange juice spruced me up if just a little bit. I slung the strap of the messenger bag over my shoulder and grabbed the keys from the desk in the foyer.

The walk to my longtime hideout was in a haze of slow footsteps. I wasn't really thinking about anything in particular, but I wasn't paying attention either. Just a few minutes later I was stepping over the run down gate at the front of the field. Only as I was about a few yards from the oak tree did I notice I was not alone.

I was too far away to see who the figure belonged to, but I was close enough to know that the lean, muscular build belonged to a male. I stopped in my sluggish walk to the tree, surprised that someone was here besides me. This place was never visited by anyone. Not to get possessive or anything, but I felt comfortable calling this place mine.

The figure's head turned to look straight at me. My heart rate suddenly sped up as I saw him push off the tree and started walking toward me. My brain began to register the situation. I was in an abandoned field with a guy that could be a murderer/rapist for all I know and he was headed straight for me.

The only sensible thing to do at that moment flashed into my mind. I turned and ran. Maybe I would have gotten a little past three feet if a familiar voice hadn't called out to me.

"Brooklynn!" it said.

I stopped and looked around to the sound of my name. The guy that was now running towards me had said it. And in my moment of shock I stood rooted there long enough to see the face of the figure was Ajay's.

A wave of relief flooded me. I waited for him to come up to me.

"What are you doing here?" I asked.

"Waiting for you," he said like it was obvious.

"How'd you know I would come here?" I asked a little freaked that he knew I came here.

"I've seen you here a couple of times before," he shrugged.

"Oh," I said as I realized it was possible that he could have been walking by and spotted me here.

A short silence ensued after that. I waited to see if he had to say anything to say and when he made no move to say anything I spoke up, "well you found me, what did you want?"

He ducked his head a little as if to imply that I was missing something obvious, but as much as I tried I couldn't find out what he wanted.

"Have you forgotten our science project?" he asked.

Whoa, wait. Do I not get any time to myself? It's a Saturday for crying out loud.

But for some reason I didn't voice my thoughts to him as I felt oddly relieved, probably because I wasn't forced to be bored the rest of the day.

"Ugh, fine, let's get this over with," I said turning around and walking out of the field not waiting for Ajay to catch up.

I actually found the new turn of events relieving, disturbingly so. I couldn't really figure out why I was happy that I didn't have to spend my whole day under a tree by myself. Sure, now I had something to do that was a little more worth my time and some company, but it was Ajay. I should have told him flat out no, but I didn't.

I locked the door behind us as we stepped into the foyer, I was always cautious about locking it whenever I was alone home. And since that was more than often, it had become a subconscious habit.

I turned around to see him on the other side of the entrance hall leaning against the banister of the stairwell and it was then I had noticed his apparel. Under his thick black hoodie I could make out a band t shirt. His usual skinny jeans were adorned with a few chains dangling from his belt loop to his pocket like most guys wear it. His repetitive use of converse never surprised me but the color of this one did. It was bright pink.

Someone's making a statement

My eyebrow arched slightly as I took in his clothes especially his sneakers. A smile twitched at the corners of my mouth before I walked passed him and up the stairs. As expected he followed me to my room.

"You have a problem with my clothes?' he asked sitting, uninvited, on my bed.

As a matter of fact it was the exact opposite; his clothes gave him this sort of rebellious look that complemented his personality and I found this annoyingly . . . sexy. His confidence helped. He knew he looked hotter than most guys ever could in his garb.

I didn't bother to answer his question as I sat on the swivel chair at my desk. Silence ensued. I waited to see if he would say something and was sort of surprised when he didn't as he was so usually full of chats.

"Why are you so quiet?" I ventured to ask.

He shrugged as I had done.

I folded my arms across my chest and my stare turned into a slight glare. This lasted for about a minute before he spoke up.

"What?"

"Why are you here?" I asked suddenly realizing he must have had better things to do than sit here and work on a science project we had nearly a month to finish.

"I thought I made it clear when I said we had a-"

"Don't pull that crap with me, I know you have better things to do on a Saturday. What is it that you really want?" I had interrupted him with a snappy response.

He didn't answer which only frustrated me. I waited a few seconds until I gave up. What was the point in trying to figure him out anyway? I twirled in my chair to face my desk where I opened my laptop and booted it up.

About twenty five minutes had passed and I had almost forgotten that Ajay was in my room lounging quietly on my bed. That is until he spoke.

"What are you doing?" his voice floated through the silence.

I almost jumped. I had resorted to multitasking with the net and Word as the project thing was obviously not going to be done in this situation.

"Nothing," I said as I continued typing my poem.

"Doesn't seem like nothing," he pushed.

"Well it is," I shrugged not really paying much attention as I typed away.

A crumpled piece of paper was lying at the side of my keyboard with messy words scribbled all over it. If I remember correctly it was a poem I had written about a month ago that I kept procrastinating on. See, I usually type my poems on my computer as it made them much more personal than having them lying around in loose pages.

No one really knew of this hidden talent, not even Jamie, I mean I never felt the need to tell anyone and besides they were supposed to be personal. They were what I felt, how I expressed myself.

"What's this?" I heard his voice much closer than I remembered him being, but before I could react he had snatched the crumpled paper from the desk and began reading it.

"No!" I gasped as I jumped out of my chair and reached for the paper which he held higher as he read.

"Give it back, Ajay!" I yelled as I jumped for it.

That didn't help much as he turned around using his other hand to push me away as he continued to read. I tried to push his arm away, but it was too strong, I began to get desperate as he flipped the page over.

"Ajay!" I shouted trying my best to reach around him and rip the paper from his grasp, but to no avail.

Right as I was about to throw myself at him his arm lowered and I figured the damage was done. As his defense was down I grabbed the paper from his hands.

"You idiot, you weren't supposed to read that, that's an invasion of personal privacy!" I shouted at him with tears of fury blurring my vision.

He didn't seem to be put off by my ranting.

"Is this what you feel like?" his face seemed to hold an expression I was not expecting, something mixed with sorrow and sympathy.

Great just what I need, his pity

I turned around furiously wiping at my eyes, ignoring his query as I crumpled the paper and threw it at the waste basket.

"Is it?" he asked again obviously wanting the answer.

I didn't want to answer at all, but I knew he was just going to ask again.

"It's written on the paper isn't it?" I said bitterly.

I heard him step closer, "Brooklynn I—"

"Don't," I spat out already knowing what he was going to say.

My fury wasn't really directed at him . . . well it was, but not entirely. I was angrier with myself. I wasn't really sure why either, but I was. Besides he wasn't supposed to read it. No one was.

I felt his hand on my shoulder to which I immediately shook off.

"Don't touch me," I said in a vehemently low whisper.

"I'm sorry," he said.

"I don't want your pity, forget you ever read that, ok?" I said turning around to face him with the fury burning evidently in my eyes.

"How could I?" he asked with concern.

"You weren't supposed to read it anyway, so just erase it from your memory, and move on, let's start on the project," I said turning around and going back to my computer.

The document with the half written poem was there. I closed it off without bothering to save it, what was the point anyway. The whole idea of personal sort of flew out the window when he read it.

"So what do you think we should do, the written part is done and we need a physical experiment, I was thinking we should use people as our lab rats. Oh and Mr. Dennis gave me a questionnaire for us to fill out," I said pulling a sheet of paper from my science notebook, ignoring the look he was directing my way.

I gave it to him and he took it and skimmed over it.

Half an hour or so later we were discussing the ideas we had come up with so far. One of our few options was to video tape people's reactions to the situations they were in. And according to the list we had to get about seven video tapes illustrating the reactions when they experienced: fear, joy, pain, depression, anxiety, boredom, and anger.

"That might be a problem, what are you planning on doing, bringing a video camera to school?" I asked skeptically.

"Well the second option is to go around to different people and ask them how they react when they feel the different emotions," he said.

"Hmm, it isn't as exciting as the video tape, but, yeah, it's a good idea."

"Why don't we combine the two? Get a few videos if we can and also have people tell us," he said.

We agreed on that idea and but then hunger stepped in cutting our brainstorming short.

He sat at the bar while I tried to figure out what I should make for the both of us to eat. I wasn't big on cooking, but it seemed like I would have to resort to pulling out the raw ingredients and a pan.

"Pasta sounds good?" I asked.

He nodded as he sat back in his stool, "you cook?"

"When the time calls for it, sure," I said as I grabbed a can of sauce and a pack of macaroni from the cupboard.

I got everything ready while we just chatted lightly. As I put the spaghetti to cook I leaned against the counter.

"I bet I can cook better than you," he said spontaneously.

"Excuse me?" I said not sure I heard him right.

"I can cook better than you," he repeated smugly.

"How are you so sure, you haven't even tasted my cooking," I said.

"And I am not going to," he said as he stood up and rounded the island to stand beside me on the other side of the kitchen.

"What do you-what are you doing?" I asked as he nudged me aside and began opening cupboards.

"Where're your seasonings?" he asked.

"Over there," I pointed to a cupboard above the stove.

He went over to the said cabinet and pulled out three or so bottles of different spices. Then he went to the fridge and brought out a handful of green stuff, I couldn't really see what he had in his hand so I couldn't identify it clearly.

After a few seconds of him gathering extra ingredients I just retired to the stool he had left at the bar as I watched him prepare our lunch. When he had finished most of whatever he was doing and was just stirring the pot I ventured to ask what it was that he had done to the food I was supposed to eat.

"So, where did you learn to cook?" I asked the first question that came to mind.

"Television; food network really goes to good use," he said as he leaned against the counter like I had done.

"Hmm," I said.

"Why'd you bother to learn?" I asked.

"My parents aren't there and I have to feed myself," he stated.

This led to me asking another question, but before I could open my mouth to ask he beat me too it.

"What is this, twenty questions?" he asked amused.

"Maybe," I replied.

"Well then I get to ask questions too," he said.

"Sure, but me first, where are your parents then?"

"Dead."

Oh . . .

I didn't really know what to say to that, I am pretty sure he didn't want to hear that I was sorry. My gaze fell and my face colored in the awkwardness of the moment that followed.

"Don't worry, you didn't know," he said relieving the tension that was building, "My turn to ask two questions, where is your mom?"

"At work."

"On a Saturday?"

"She's a lawyer."

"And the second one, why is your dad never here?" he asked.

"I don't have one" I answered.

He gave me a questionable glance.

"Left my mother during pregnancy," I half lied.

He nodded as he heard my reply.

"Can I ask another one?" he asked folding his arms across his chest.

"You just did, but go ahead," I allowed.

"Was it true?" he asked softly.

"Huh?" I was confused by his vagueness.

"The poem; was it true?" he asked looking me directly in the eyes, which I cut short by looking down.

Ugh! I thought this was behind us. What happened to him erasing his memory?

"I-um," I stuttered looking for a way not to answer him.

"Just answer," he said softly.

"Why should I?" I queried suddenly curious as to why he wouldn't just leave the subject alone.

He sighed as he looked down briefly, "Why don't you just answer the question?"

"It's my business, why should I share it with you?" I snapped although I wasn't sure why, his persistence was irritating me.

"Because I care," he answered.

"Please," I scoffed, "you really expect me to believe that?"

"Yes, why not?" he asked with evident hurt in his voice.

Is he serious? Does he really expect me for one moment to believe that he cares?

Not having a proper response I just rolled my eyes and left the kitchen.

I was about to go into the living room when his voice called to me.

"Where are you going?"

"Nowhere," I answered as I plopped ungracefully down on the couch and turned on the TV.

I began surfing through the channels but didn't get far because all of a sudden a blur of black was placed in my line of vision.

"What?" I demanded looking up at his frustrated face. His arms were crossed and he was lightly glaring down at me.

"You really think I don't care?" he more stated than asked.

"No, I know you don't, you have no reason to," I expected him to move now that I gave him an answer but that wasn't the case.

"Ajay, move," I began to get irritated as I heard one of my favorite songs start to play and I couldn't get to see the music video for it.

His arms unfolded as he turned around and switched off the television.

"What the hell is your problem? I was watching that!" I shouted, infuriated not so much at the fact that he switched it off while I was watching it, but because he wouldn't leave me alone.

"My problem? What's yours?" he shouted back at me, "How could you honestly think that I don't care?"

"Are you serious? You're Ajay Edison for crying out loud, the school's bad boy, everyone knows who you are, and you don't care for anyone but yourself!" I half yelled the obvious.

His fierce gaze died instantly as he looked at me with hurt and betrayal residing in his beautiful green eyes.

"Is that what you think of me, I thought you knew me better than that," he said softly.

I sighed as I realized what he said was true, I did know him a little better than I used to and I knew that the charade he put on wasn't entirely who he was.

"Look, I'm sorry, but even so, you hardly know me . . ."

"Don't even pull that card Brooklynn," he interrupted me, "I know you better than a lot of people do," he spoke the truth once again.

And I couldn't argue because he was undoubtedly right, we had spent a lot of time talking and getting to know each other better that other night. But still, I wasn't going to sit here and let myself believe that he cared.

A short silence ensued before he spoke softly.

"Just answer the question, please Brooklynn," he said staring into my eyes.

I sighed before I muttered an inaudible answer.

"What?" he asked coming closer.

"Yes," I said softly but loud enough for him to hear.

I wasn't at all expecting his next response.

"Can I see?"

I looked up incredulously.

"What?"

"Can I see?" he asked again.

"I answered your question, wasn't that enough?"

His only reply was to look questioningly into my eyes.

I dropped my gaze, but I didn't answer. Some time past before he stepped closer, taking my silence as permission, and took my hand in his. He hesitated a moment before he took his other had and rolled up my sleeve, letting out surprised gasps, before stopping at my elbow.

I looked up slightly to see that his horrified gaze was firmly planted on my forearm.

"Why?"

This was the part I hated. The reason no one else knew. I couldn't answer him. I didn't have an answer anyway. I myself wondered why. 'It's complicated' doesn't cover it. Complicated was an understatement.

I pulled my hand from his grasp and rolled the sleeve back into place over my arm. His gaze lingered for a moment before it looked up to reach mine.

Before I could even register what had happened, his warm and comforting arms were around me in a firm hug. I was stiff at first, but relaxed after a few seconds grateful for the unasked questions and comfort he provided.

For those few pleasant moments that the hug lasted it didn't matter who was hugging me. All I knew was that I wasn't alone, a feeling I was beginning to get used to, an experience I was starting to like.

This is nice. Whoever thought that Ajay would be the one to comfort me?

You are so hard headed you know that, I have . . .

Why do you keep popping up in my head?!

I'm your conscience, I never leave

Well you're beginning to get . . .

I pulled from Ajay's grasp as the toxic scent of smoke entered my nostrils. It took me only a half a second to figure out the problem. I dashed into the kitchen to see the steel pot bubbling over and puffs of smoke seeping from the creases of the lid.

I ran to the stove and slid the pot over to a dormant burner while unplugging the smoke detector overhead to prevent the alarm from going off. As the smoke cleared I lifted the pot to see all the water had evaporated and the noodles had stuck to the bottom of the pot, burned.

"Well there goes our lunch," I muttered as I poked the burnt noodles with a spoon.

"Oops," I heard a guilty voice behind me.

I turned around to see Ajay standing in the doorway looking sheepishly at me, biting his lower lip.

"Don't worry, I'll just order pizza," I said as I dumped the pot into the sink and picked up the phone.

I called my favorite pizzeria and also the closest, and made the same order I made every time, seeing that that topping was my favorite and Ajay had liked it as well.

I put the phone back on its cradle and turned to see Ajay scrubbing at the pot I had put in the sink.

"What are you doing?" I asked leaning against the countertop.

"Washing the dishes, what else?"

"Um, why?" I asked.

"It's my fault our lunch burned so I think I should make up for that," he explained as he dried off the pot and put it in the cupboard it had come from.

"I think you did that on purpose, because you know you can't cook," I joked.

"Excuse me, you think I can't cook?" he asked incredulously.

I just laughed at the look he was giving me.

"Well how am I supposed to know, you offered to cook, and end up burning the food, doesn't that say it all?" I asked amused.

"That says nothing. It was an accident," he muttered crossing his arms over his chest.

I glanced at him and couldn't help, but burst out into a fit of giggles. The way he looked like a child who had just been denied a cookie before dinner. It was hilarious, well at least in my eyes because Ajay didn't seem to think so as he glared at me while I fell to the floor clutching my sides.

My laughing died and I recollected my composure. I stood up and mumbled a soft sorry between giggles.

He just rolled his eyes and walked into the living room with me not far behind. He sat on the couch leaving room for me as he switched on the

TV. He started flipping channels until he would reach a certain channel that held my interest then began zipping through again.

I wasn't sure if he was a really indecisive person or if he was just doing it to make me annoyed, but he kept stopping at channels and when they gained my interest he would suddenly change the channel again.

I groaned inwardly as he switched from Harry Potter to another channel. Out of the corner of my eye I saw his mouth twitch into an amused smirk.

That little twit, so he was doing it on purpose. Without warning I lunged myself onto him and grabbed the remote. With him not expecting my sudden attack I got a hold of it effortlessly. What happened next caught me off guard; both of us fell off the sofa and onto the soft rug with a loud thud. The remote flew from my hands and skidded across the wooden linoleum floor.

Both of our heads shot up towards the contraption. Not waiting for him to act I pushed myself off the floor and went for the remote, but before I could even move a step further, his fingerless-gloved hand wrapped around my ankle, being the cause for me reuniting with the floor. He took that as his advantage and crawled quickly for the remote.

To an onlooker this would look like the human version to the fights you normally viewed on Animal Planet when predators are fighting for their prey; the difference was that this scene was less violent and a lot more hilarious.

"Give me the remote!" I growled as his hands wrapped around it.

"No, I'm the guest, we watch what I want," he said cradling the thing to his chest.

"It's my house, my rules, give it to me," I said getting up and walking towards him.

"No!" he said before he ran behind the sofa.

My eyes narrowed as I stared at him. My breathing was still heavy from all the trouble of trying to get the damned remote control.

I began walking slowly to the couch. As I got close enough to it that I could touch it I stopped glaring slightly at him as he smiled lopsidedly still holding it to his chest.

"I'm going to ask you one more time," I said slowly, collecting my breath.

"No," he stated before I could even ask.

Oh well . . .

I jumped onto the sofa and flew at him knocking him to the floor.

"Oomph!" was all he uttered as I grabbed the remote and ran back to the TV laughing manically. I didn't pause to wonder why the TV was off as I pressed the power button to switch it back on. Nothing . . . I pressed it again, this time aiming directly at the screen and with a little more force.

"What the?" I asked myself as I pressed it again.

Why the hell wasn't it coming on? I began to get frustrated as I tried again. As I was about to press it one more time a shout of laughter filled my ears. I turned around to see Ajay on the floor rolling around, clutching at his sides in laughter.

"What did you do?" I asked narrowing my eyes at him.

"Me? Don't you mean the power company?" he asked between fits of laughter.

It took me a slow second to realize what he was implying as I became aware of the unusually still silence we were enveloped in. The hum of all the electronic appliances ceased to add life to the already empty house.

Power's out

No really I hadn't noticed.

Shut up.

"Now what?" I asked as I sat on the floor beside his laughing body.

Before he could answer there was a rapid knock on the door.

"Food!" he said getting up and going to answer the door.

I also stood up going to the kitchen to take some money to pay the delivery guy.

"Don't eat all," I said as I passed Ajay with the box already opened in the living room.

I jogged to the front door where the guy was standing there looking sort of confused.

"Sorry about that," I said giving him a twenty and telling him to keep the change.

I came back into the living room to see that two slices were already gone from the box and he was reaching for his third.

"Hey!" I slapped his hand away as I took the box from him.

"I'm hungry!" he protested.

"So am I," I replied as I took the box into the kitchen with him following a few steps behind.

I set the box on the island and took a plate out of its shelf. I took four slices out of the box and placed them onto the plate afterwards sliding the box with the rest of the pizza towards him. He accepted and reached for another slice greedily while I took out some condiments and squirted them onto my pizza.

This time I didn't make him turn around as I ate because I felt more comfortable around him than I used to. And I hated to admit it but his presence was something I enjoyed.

During my second slice of pizza his voice broke the unnatural silence—due to the power still being out and all.

"What would you say if I asked to spend the night here again?" he queried looking me directly in the eyes. Something I noticed he did when he was being serious.

"I'd only know if you asked," I said with a lift of my shoulder.

"Ok then can I spend the night?"

I stopped mid bite. I wasn't really expecting him to ask. I thought it was just a random, hypothetical question. What was I going to say now?

Yes!

Why?

Hello, why not?! He's being polite about it and he looks like he wants to stay!

I paused before I nodded.

"Thanks, I'll go get my stuff," he said standing up taking the empty box and throwing it in the bin.

I stood up also and put my last slice of pizza in the fridge.

"Wanna come?" he asked.

"Sure," I answered with a slight smile.

I grabbed my jacket from the coat closet along with my keys and followed him out the door into the cool November air and locked the door behind us.

"Can we stay up late tonight?" he asked like a little kid would as we turned away from my street.

"Um, ok," I answered.

"And watch, movies?" he inquired with an innocent gleam in his eye.

"If the power comes back on then sure."

I was slightly surprised at the light atmosphere between us after what had happened before, with me showing him the faded lacerations on my arm. I still couldn't get over the fact that I had given him a peek at the secrets of my life. What had gotten into me? Why was I suddenly feeling a certain bond with Ajay? Wasn't this the same boy I had no intentions of ever getting close to in the beginning?

I shook away the thoughts as I focused on my present surroundings.

We continued our walk to his house slowly starting a light conversation. Before I knew it he turned up the pathway that led to his house. I was so busy laughing at the joke he made a few seconds ago that I barely noticed we had reached. I turned a second after and followed up the path to his house where he was already through the door. I walked in after him, closing and locking the door behind me still with the subconscious caution I had with locking doors.

This time was the second time I ever came into his house and since I was I much more at ease than the last time I was here and I could stop and take in my surroundings. His house had that industrial look to it, all the furniture took on the shape of a square of some sort. The walls were brick and if you looked up you could see the ventilation system running around the house. I liked the feeling the atmosphere presented to me. I felt more at home than I did in my own house and I find that not surprising in the least.

I looked around before I followed him upstairs catching up to him as I saw him turn into his room at the end of the hallway. I was slower as I took in the house.

He lived here by himself according to what he told me, and it seemed like it was well kept, better than I imagined a house owned by an orphaned 18 year-old would be.

I walked into his room as I came to the open door at the end of the hallway. This room was different from the rest of the house and very different from how I'd imagined it being five minutes ago as I worked my way up to his room. The walls weren't brick like the rest of the house's interior; in fact they were black and pink from the choreographed wallpaper.

In the left corner under a circular window was his bed, I had a slight urge to go over and sit on it. The duvet looked so inviting; it looked to be silk or something equally luxurious and soft. He must have a hard time getting up on mornings to go to school. I know I would with a bed as inviting as his.

"Make yourself at home," he said, pulling me out of my thoughts.

I walked over to the bed and sat down, not disappointed at all at the warmth and comfort it provided. I watched silently as he walked from his closet to his bureau, pulling different articles of clothing and other stuff.

"So?" I asked dragging the 'o' as to imply that I wanted to start a conversation.

It had been silent since we entered the house and his shuffling back and forth didn't help the silent atmosphere.

He didn't stop though as he answered, "so what?"

I sighed neglecting the intention to start a conversation and lay back on his comfortable bed with a relaxed sigh.

"Your bed is really comfortable," I stated moving my arms up and down along the satiny feel of the sheets.

"Yeah," he said as he grabbed a bag to put all the things he had taken up.

I didn't even get time to drift out of consciousness as I heard him calling my name.

"Come on Brooklynn!"

"Mm, five minutes," I protested as I curled myself into the embrace of the bed.

"C'mon, let's go," he said tugging lightly on my arm giving me no other choice but to get up, but not without a groan of dissatisfaction.

I waited on the small porch as he locked the door behind us, "Your house is really well kept, I never thought of you as a neat freak," there were a lot of things he was surprising me with lately.

"I try," he shrugged with a small smile. It was sometime after eight, I wasn't really too sure about the time. But I was sure about the fun I was currently having.

One step at a time . . . just a little bit closer. I slowly reached my hands out and pushed the door having it make an annoyingly loud creak as it swung forward into the room.

Silence. I hesitated before I cautiously placed one foot in front of the other in a timid walk. I could barely see more than a foot in front of my face. I wasn't so worried about walking blindly as I was about not knowing where he was.

I took another step into the room looking around although it did me no good, I could just make out the outline of a table in front of me.

Ok nothing here-wait what was that?

I froze mid step as I heard the unmistakable sound of someone shuffling. I was definitely not alone. The only problem was where he was. I moved even stealthier if that's possible along the wall. I was not about to let him surprise me. I was determined to win.

There it was again, that sound.

There was no mistake this time as to where it was coming from. I spun around about to pounce not in the least bit expecting the eerie sight I was faced with.

My frightened scream was drowned out halfway by uncontrolled laughing.

My horror stricken face instantly morphed into a scowl. I had lost, again, to him. How was it that he kept winning? One would swear he had some freak night vision or something. This was our fourth round and his third time at catching me off guard at flashlight tag. It wasn't fair that the power was still out and it was dark everywhere, he had the element of surprise on his side!

I waited, with a hand on my hip, for him to finish his uncontrolled laughter.

"You are so easy to scare!" he stated which earned him another glare which I was sure he couldn't see anyway.

"Whatever," I said walking past him and out of the room, "I quit."

"Aw, c'mon, we only played four times and you never even caught me," he whined.

"Exactly, you're . . . undefeatable, let's call it quits," I said still walking away.

I could hear his footsteps padding softly behind me as he followed.

"Fine, where are you going?" he asked.

"I'm hungry," I answered heading for the kitchen.

I switched on my flashlight as I waved it around the room. I walked straight to the counter in the far left and climbed up on it to open the ridiculously high cupboard above it.

Either I was just short or the architecture in this kitchen was designed for the abnormally tall. But before I could reach my hand for the bag of Cheddar Combos his pale hand beat me to it, pulling it out and resting it on the counter beside my knees.

I was beginning to think I was just short.

I mumbled thanks as I hopped from the countertop and onto the floor beside him.

"Combos?" he asked eyeing the bag with disapproving speculation.

"Yes," I grabbed the bag from him and held it to my chest protectively, "what's wrong with Combos?"

He paused for a moment before answering, "Nothing, I guessed you might want something a little more fulfilling."

"Well if you hadn't noticed, power's gone so I can't really make lasagna and Crème Brûlée, now can I?" I questioned sarcastically.

"Hm, well at least let's make something," he said.

"Like what, the stove's electric," I answered.

"Whoever said we had to use a stove?"

I raised an eyebrow, questioning his sanity.

"Well what other alternative do you have?"

For a second I heard shuffling then I could see his hands in his pockets. Not two seconds later they returned with an object.

Before I could register what had happened, a sudden flicker of light illuminated our faces.

Realization hit.

"Wait, no way!"

"Why not?" he cut me off.

"Are you really serious? What are you going to do? Wait for it to heat up the food, that'd take forever," I said trying to knock some sense in his testosterone ridden mind.

"Marshmallows would cook in, like, two seconds," he said flicking the lighter again when the light had flickered out.

I stopped as I realized he was right. I suddenly felt jealous that I hadn't thought of that first.

I turned around and pulled a bag of marshmallows out of the cupboard along with two skewers from the draw that held most of our cutlery.

"Ok," I paused, "c'mon," I said walking towards the living room where I sat on the plush rug waiting for him to follow suit.

I handed him a metal skewer and kept one for myself as I opened the bag. I took one out and placed it at the edge of my skewer to which he followed.

He flicked the light on again and it dawned on me that he was walking around with a lighter which meant he obviously used it for something.

"You smoke?" it sounded more like an accusation, as I already knew the answer to that, I had seen him at the back of school torturing his lungs on those cancer sticks many times before.

He just nodded as he allowed his marshmallow to be licked hungrily by the small flame.

I watched it turn brown then blacken at the edges as I asked, "Why?"

He didn't answer as he pulled away his skewer and blew on the hot spongy candy.

I placed mine over the flame to let it take on the same fate. It was silent for a moment as we were both lost in our own thoughts.

He smokes, I hate to see people, especially young people, waste away their health on those nicotine wraps.

For once I sort of agree with you

Sort of?

Well yea . . . you don't know why he does it. Could be stress, or a comfort.

Smoking is a comfort?

You're one to talk, if I'm not mistaken you find solace in cyber freaks you don't even know

Well at least I don't put my health in danger

Why do you care all of a sudden anyway?

Because I . . .

Why did I care? Since when did I ever care what happened to him? When did the line between friend and enemy suddenly dissolve?

I was knocked out of my thoughts as he flicked the light back on as it had blown out. I looked up and couldn't help but stare at his face, illuminated by the dull glow of the lone flame. His eyes were always the first to catch my attention. Looking at his eyes I could see the difference between the Ajay everyone thinks they know and the one I got the chance to.

And my quarrelling thoughts subsided. He wasn't who I and everyone else thought him to be. He had a personality that most didn't know of. He was a person I liked, my friend.

"You really shouldn't, it's bad for you."

I am pretty sure he already knew that . . .

His only reply was to stare at the dancing flame before us. Coming to terms that I wasn't going to get a response I switched the topic to something a lot more optimistic.

"What are you planning to do tomorrow?" I asked having nothing better to put forward.

He was silent for a few seconds before he spoke, "There's a party at Tristan's house tomorrow night, I was thinking of going to that."

A picture of Ajay's best friend popped into my mind, dark brown hair blue eyes, school heartthrob.

I nodded as another picture replaced the one of Tristan, heavy music, sweaty people dancing and having a great time, a scene that wasn't at all difficult to picture Ajay in.

"I was also thinking, of asking you to accompany me," he said looking directly at me, his features dully illuminated by the flickering flame.

Did he just . . . ?

"So will you . . . ?"

Yes he did!

His gaze never faltered as he stared at me. He had just asked me to a party with him!

"Why?" I blurted out the first thing that came to mind.

"Because you're my friend and I want you to come with me," he answered never removing his eyes from my own.

Wow, he admitted it. I guess the feeling is mutual. We were friends. I thought about his proposal for a few seconds, weighing the cons and pros. I wanted so badly to accept his offer and there didn't seem to be any drawbacks to saying yes, so I did.

"Great, I'll pick you up at six," he said returning his gaze to the lighter in front of him.

I smiled in return although he couldn't see it, but I was so happy. My gaze turned towards the flame as well and I realized that the marshmallows were finished and we were just enjoying the little light that the flame provided.

At first I thought it was my vision going dim but after blinking rapidly a few times I realized the lighter was dying. The fuel was running out. And no more than five seconds later we were once again plunged into total darkness.

"What now?" his voice startled me.

"Um, what do you want to do?" I asked not having an answer.

There were limited things one can do when the power went out.

"I'm not sleepy yet," he replied.

"Neither am I," that was somewhat a lie as I was feeling a little tired, but not enough to want to sleep.

Silence settled again.

"What time is it?" I mumbled half to myself.

"Almost ten," he answered after glancing at his watch.

"Let's talk," I suddenly offered right out of the blue.

"About?" he asked.

"Anything, ask me a question and I'll answer."

"Is this another game of 'This or That'?" he asked skeptically.

"No, this is just a conversation between two friends who want to know more about each other," I replied hoping he would just go with the flow.

"Ok, when's your birthday?"

"December 8th," I answered automatically, "Yours?"

"November 13th," he answered, "What's the limit to these questions, can I ask you anything I want?" he queried leaning back on his elbows.

"If I don't like the question I won't answer," I replied.

"Fair enough, what's your biggest fear, other than bugs I mean?" he added.

"Who said I was afraid of bugs?" I asked, a little annoyed at the sexism, "My biggest fear would have to be . . . falling in love," I answered.

His only reply was to stare at me in shock, "You're afraid of falling in love . . . why?"

I shrugged before answering, "I've seen what it does to people and I don't want it happening to me."

"What exactly has it done?" he interrogated.

"It lies, hurts and ruins people," I answered.

"You haven't seen the other side of it then, if that's all you can come up with."

"I don't want to. You appear to know a lot with the way you're talking."

"So do you," he answered with a smirk playing on his lips.

The topic was tottering a little on the uncomfortable side so I quickly asked him a question.

"What're your greatest dreams and desires?" I quizzed wanting to know what motivated him the most.

He paused for a moment apparently debating the question in his head.

"You know I've never really asked myself that question, there are a whole lot of things I want in life, but I guess the one thing I'm truly after is . . . happiness. No matter what I'm doing, where I am, or who I'm with, I just want to be happy."

I found myself smiling at his heartfelt reply. This was the side I loved to see, the side where he was honest with himself and didn't put of a façade to fool anyone else.

"What about you, what do you want most?" he turned the question on me.

A bigger, yet self-conscious smile found itself upon my lips, "This might surprise you, but I want so badly to be an actress, always have, ever since I can remember," I said looking down the entire time not wanting to face the look of judgment on his face that was sure to be there.

"An actress?" he inquired.

"Yes, I know it's stupid, but . . ."

"It's not stupid at all, why would you think that?"

"Because, it's true, it's not like that dream's gonna come true," I stated the obvious.

"What are you talking about, why would you say something like that?" he sounded offended like I had insulted him in some way.

I didn't bother to answer; I knew it wasn't going to happen. There were millions of other people who had that same dream and I was no one special. What made me different from all the others? What made me better than all those pretty, smart and way more outgoing girls? Nothing. The show biz industry would quicker select them than me. They had what it took, I just had the dream, and you need more than just a dream to make it.

"I don't ever want to hear you saying that again, stop being negative, you can do anything you want to," his voice sounded closer than it was.

I looked up to see him crawling over to sit next to me. Seconds later his familiar warmth surrounded me in a hug.

I hugged back, but I didn't answer. He just said it because he felt the need to. Besides, how could he be so sure? He'd never seen me act. He didn't know if I even could, but deep down I knew I was good, great even, at acting. It was one of my very few talents, it was my calling. But, no matter how good I was at this, I knew there were people better.

Our little conversation continued with us asking questions and I was happy that Ajay didn't remove his arms from around me.

I'm not sure what time it was that I drifted off to sleep but I knew it was sometime after midnight.

My eyes dropped closed leaving all the new knowledge I had on Ajay to sink in as I slept.

November 19—Sunday

What was I supposed to wear? I mean it's not like I went to parties every weekend. In fact I can only remember one party I ever attended and that was one when I was six. A kid in my class had a birthday splash and I was invited, but I am pretty sure the party I was going to now didn't have laughing clowns and I wasn't supposed to wear a pink puffy dress with my hair in two pigtails.

I opened my closet and went to the side that I rarely used. I never thought that all these designer clothes would ever come in handy. I searched through all the clothes until I came to a classic little black dress and simple black heels. I didn't know what the atmosphere of the party would be like but I felt confident that the dress would fit right in as it was neither casual nor over the top.

I laid the dress gently on my bed before I walked to my adjacent bathroom, to shower and get ready.

Nearly an hour later I was wrapped in a towel applying lip-gloss and a thin line of eyeliner, nothing much, but it was the most makeup I ever wore. Deciding I looked decent enough I walked back into my room and began putting on my wear for the night. When I looked in the mirror I was a little surprised at the person staring back. It was the same person, it's just that I looked different, maybe even, dare I say, pretty.

Now what was I to do with my hair? It looked so bland when I left it down like I had it all the time. I decided to tie half up and left a few tendrils to flirt with my face. Feeling to do just a little bit more I took out the curling iron that I never used and curled random sections making it look all mixed up and pretty. When I was done I stepped back and gazed into the mirror.

The girl in the reflection staring back held a timid stance with unsure eyes. How could she not? This was something new for her. Going to a party with people and socializing, it was all foreign.

I nearly tripped over my own feet as I heard the doorbell ring. I glanced at the clock on the wall and saw that it was three minutes to 6. I grabbed a twenty dollar bill just in case and placed it in my bra seeing that I had no pockets and I don't use purses. Too much luggage.

I left my room and slowly made my way downstairs to answer the front door. What if Ajay decided he didn't want to take me anymore, what if I looked ugly?

I stemmed those thoughts as I reached out a shaking hand and opened the door.

"Hey, re-" he stopped short as he caught sight of me.

I immediately felt self-conscious as a blush crawled up my neck.

"What?" I asked timidly wondering if maybe I had something on my face.

"N-nothing, you look great," he, for the first time ever, stammered, while looking me in the eyes.

"Thank you, so do you," I didn't lie, he was even more gorgeous than usual.

I didn't think that was possible, but taking in the black, button-up, dress shirt paired with dark blue pencil jeans, pink converse and pink and black striped fingerless gloves, he proved me wrong.

"Shall we get going milady?" he asked playfully as he linked his arm with mine.

"Yes we shall," I replied already beginning to lose the previous nervous feelings.

It was hard to feel shy around him now after spending so much time with him and learning so much about him. As we walked towards the street I noticed a black Audi parked in front of the driveway. It never occurred to me that he had a car before now and to be honest I was already in love with it. I have a thing for Audis, I'm not a car expert or anything, but I just love Audis. He opened my door for me as we got to the passenger side then went around getting in himself.

"You have an Audi A6?" I asked incredulously although the answer was an obvious yes.

"You are so lucky," I gushed as he started the car and pulled away from the curb.

"Thanks," he said keeping his eyes on the road.

"How come I've never seen it before?" I wanted to know.

The two times I had been at his house I had never seen this car, but I hadn't been to the garage so it was plausible.

He merely shrugged as he answered, "Well I don't need to use it much so . . ." he trailed off letting the sentence hang, leaving the message to be caught on.

I nodded whilst I leaned back into the cool embrace of the beige leather seat. The ride was short and filled with a comfortable silence that broke when we pulled up to the house. It was huge, like titanic huge. This boy's family obviously owned money and lots of it to be able to buy a mansion that magnitude. My jaw loosened in awe as I took in the size of the building, the second thing I noticed was the number of cars parked along the long driveway and the amount of people milling around outside. I could only imagine how much more of them were inside

This was the part I wasn't so excited about, but since there were so many of them it wouldn't be hard to blend into a crowd and not worry about being confronted.

"Ok, stay with me at all times, and if you do get lost, don't accept anything from anyone!" Ajay began as he parked, but I cut him off . . .

"I know, don't talk to any strangers and don't take candy from anyone who offers it; I'm not five Ajay."

He rolled his eyes, "I know, it's just that I don't want anything happening to you. These parties can get pretty . . . wild," he explained with a pointed look.

"Thanks, I'll try to be safe," I said smiling as we both got out of the car.

I closed my door and turned around to look at the immense house ahead of me. I could see the outlines of bodies moving around through the large windows on both floors and I could hear the music that was blasting from within those walls.

I looked to my side as Ajay came up beside me with a casual smirk. He took my hand and began leading me towards our night's adventures.

The music was unbelievably deafening to the point where I felt the bass beats surge through by body, yet I couldn't distinguish the angst ridden words coming from the singer's screams.

Everything was going fine, until I had managed to lose Ajay. It wasn't hard either, having bodies grinding into us, disconnecting our hands and it didn't help either that everyone decided to wear black or some dark color otherwise.

So now I was just being guided by the dancing bodies, trying not to panic, maybe even try to enjoy myself, because I had given up trying to find him a long time ago. It started to get frustrating when I realized the back of almost every boy's head was styled in that same 'scene' manner. It was like I was in the middle of a sea of black clothed clones.

I began to feel lost when everywhere I turned was the same picture, until a stairwell caught my eye. I fought against the dancing current to make my way over the staircase, pushing and squeezing myself in between raving people.

When I made it to the stairs I noticed that it was deserted except for a few couples going up to, I assumed, find vacant bedrooms. I followed after them having no choice, not wanting to be devoured by that mass of people downstairs again.

The music was less intense, not really quieter, but less. I let out a shaky breath I wasn't even aware I was holding and continued along the wide corridor. I wasn't sure exactly where I was headed, but I didn't turn back or stop either.

The house was bigger than I gave it credit for, the hallways sort of reminded me of a hotel, long and never ending. Not finding anything worth looking for and remembering I was looking for Ajay I decided to turn back, but that was until I heard a few voices down the hall.

Having nothing better to do and my curiosity tickled, I tiptoed towards the sound of the conversation. I went up against the door and pressed my ear to the wood to hear more clearly, and though I knew this was eavesdropping and it was considered bad I couldn't help it.

Not really expecting much you can imagine my relief when I recognized one of the voices to be Ajay's. The other voice surprised me greatly. I was positive I wasn't mistaken; the other voice had to belong to Jamie.

I was about to knock and make my presence known when I heard the next line.

"So you used Brooklynn, to get to me?" Jamie sounded furious, "If you wanted to know, you could have just asked me Ajay!"

I furrowed my eyebrows in confusion and slight hurt. Although that's all I had heard something inside of me sank.

What did she mean? He used me?

But before I could sort out my thoughts the conversation went on.

"You were avoiding me Jamie, how else was I supposed to know?" he answered.

Know what? And why didn't he deny it? Did he use me? Wait, use me for what?

"Because I was scared, we broke up and I thought you didn't want anything to do with me anymore," her voice was quieter but still loud enough for me to hear clearly.

My eyes widened in shock and realization.

Ajay and Jamie . . . together. He was who Jamie was talking about? Her ex boyfriend? Wait, that means-

"It's my child too, how long did you plan on hiding that from me, Jamie? When were you going to let me know you were pregnant?"

I couldn't breathe, I would have choked maybe, but there was nothing to choke on, not even air. I couldn't breathe; all I did was keep against the door and listen to their conversation roll along. My thoughts couldn't quite register any emotion I should have been feeling yet.

"When were you going to tell me, you were using Brooklynn?" she shot back!

"I wasn't using . . ." he began only to be cut off.

"Like hell you weren't, you didn't think I'd find out?" she snapped, "I'm sorry, I should have told you, but what you did was low Ajay, how do you think she's going to feel when she finds out?"

"When?" he asked.

"What, you think I'm going to keep this from her? She's been hurt enough as it is, I'm not going to sit back and watch you hurt my best friend more," she told him with a tone of solemnity.

I knew I should have run or something to hide myself when I heard footsteps headed towards the door I was leaning against, but I couldn't really move. The door opened and a surprised gasp left Jamie's lips. Her eyes widened slightly before she took into consideration that I was eavesdropping and probably heard most of their conversation. I looked past her to see two other occupants of the room. Ajay stood looking at me with guilt and surprise while next to him was the host of the party Tristan. I wasn't sure where he fit in to any of this, nor did I care at that moment.

Maybe I should have stayed and yelled or caused a scene, vented the emotions that were spilling over inside of me. I should have shouted at Ajay, accused him or something, tried to make sense of the whole situation, but all I did was turn around quietly and leave.

The anger, the hurt, the pain, yeah it was all there, but the most overpowering one was a feeling of disappointment, no matter how hard I tried to feel angry, I just felt foolish and disappointed . . . in myself. I know my emotions are a bit messed up, but I couldn't help it.

Why did I let myself believe that he was sincere? As much as I wanted to hate him for crushing me, I couldn't help but hate myself more, for letting him.

My vision was blurry, as I rushed through the madly dancing people. The front door came closer with every step I took and I pushed harder, not bothering to apologize when I knocked people out of my way, they didn't seem to notice though, probably too intoxicated to care.

When I broke free of the house and all its raving occupants I realized I had no idea where I would go from there. I had come with Ajay, in his car. I didn't let that stop me though as I blindly ran down the long driveway.

"Brooklynn!" I didn't bother to turn around or acknowledge the voice.

I kept my quick pace towards the road, where I was sure if I walked far enough I would be lucky to get a taxi or the bus.

"Brooklynn, wait!" the voice was closer now; still I didn't let that hinder me.

"Brook-" the voice was cut off, this time against my will I turned around.

I couldn't ignore the only person who in this whole mess apparently cared for me genuinely. I turned back and approached Jamie who was bending over slightly trying to catch her breath from running after me.

"I can give you a ride home," she said between breaths.

I helped her to stand properly when she regained her balance of oxygen.

"Don't go hurting my nephew now," I smiled faintly through the tears.

She returned that with a smile, "come on, we can go back to my place, you can stay the night."

I didn't object as I followed her to her car that was parked inconspicuously in line with the rest of the other cars lined up in the driveway.

It was a humble blue Honda Civic. We climbed in and began the trip back to her house. The ride consisted of silence, not the strained or awkward one, but not really comfortable either. The essence of confrontation was lingering, we just chose to ignore it for the time being.

Mrs. Austin was more than delighted when she learned that I was staying the night. After our late dinner, Jamie and I excused ourselves to her room.

Before the door had even closed behind us she had turned to me, "I didn't know, I'm sorry I didn't tell you who the father was, I didn't know that you and he were-"

"It's alright Jamie, really it is, that was your personal business you didn't have to tell me anything," I added a small smile to add to the attempted assurance.

"No, it's not alright, I never knew you two talked, I should have told you that he's . . . I really didn't mean to keep this from you," she explained, not bothering with my previous remark.

It wasn't her fault at all. She had no idea that Ajay and I knew each other in any way. She had all rights to keep the information about her baby's father confidential. Who could blame her, from what I figured out; it was a secret relationship to begin with. Don't ask me how I know that, gossip travels, okay? So anyway, some people may know she was preggers but no one knew who exactly the father was, and if word got out that she was in a relationship with the school's notorious delinquent then it would soil her 'good girl' reputation. I just couldn't help but feel a little stung that she didn't trust me to keep that a secret.

"Jamie, really, I don't blame you at all," I said looking her straight in the eyes hoping she would see the truth in that statement and stop going on and on blaming herself when there was no need.

She paused taking in what I just told her before she continued again, "That bastard! All he had to do was ask, I would have told him!" she fumed.

I walked past her and sat on her bed letting my head fall back. Was it true? Did he use me? I mean he didn't deny it, but then again he didn't own up to it either. Who was I kidding? What other motive would he have for talking to me then?

The science project . . .

He started before that, remember? He came to my house unexpectedly just to talk to me, and then he brought me to his house just to ask why I didn't eat in the cafeteria . . . how could I have been so stupid? It was so obvious!

Surprisingly that annoying counterpart of mine didn't have a witty response as usual, but that just finalized how irrational I had been for being so close to trusting Ajay.

"I'll deal with him when we get to school tomorrow," Jamie's voice broke through my thoughts.

"Don't bother, I don't want to turn you against him," I said honestly not wanting to get in the way of Jamie and her child's father.

"Don't be ridiculous, besides you're not turning me against him, he's doing that on his own," she muttered.

I closed my eyes hoping that I could get some peace for a few seconds, but that wish was in vain considering Jamie kept ranting like a madwoman.

"Jamie! It's okay really," I sat up frustrated after a while of listening to her go on and on about the person who I wanted to hear less and less of.

"No, it's not ok Brooklynn, how can you say that?" she asked bewildered.

"This is not something I wanna dwell on. Can we just not talk about it?" I asked tiredly, she looked like she was going to flip out so I added, "At least not now, I just want to sleep, and I've had a really long night."

She sighed in defeat and I knew she would drop the matter as of tonight. That's all I asked for. I would deal with whatever word vomit she had to spew tomorrow. Right now I just wanted to sleep it off.

She got the idea that I wanted to sleep right away so she lent me a pair of her pajamas and gave me a new toothbrush, to which I thanked her and went off to the bathroom to prepare for bed.

Sometime later, we were lying side by side in her queen sized bed just quietly murmuring, too tired to go into deep conversation.

"Are we going to school tomorrow?" she asked softly.

I thought about it for a moment, I hardly ever missed school, the last time being in the sixth grade when I got the chicken pox, so it was within reason. Was I willing to give up a day of school just because I'd been hurt by a boy? Was it really worth it? Of course not. But I was tired and worn out and school didn't seem too inviting a place to be.

"We'll skip tomorrow if that's ok with your mom," I murmured back.

I heard her shift, probably getting more comfortable, "My mom won't mind at all. So a day off tomorrow it is."

November 20—Monday

Never in my life had I been awakened in such a way. The sound of metal banging violently against metal pulled me from my slumber that morning. No matter what I did in attempt to block out the noise it wouldn't go away. Finally when my sanity could stand it no longer and it was obvious I wasn't going back to sleep that morning I sat up frustrated.

"What the hell is that racket?" I grumbled to myself.

Over on the other side of the bed Jamie's form was resting peacefully apparently undisturbed by the ridiculously loud commotion coming from downstairs.

How was it possible that she was still sleeping through all of this?

I stumbled my way out of the bed and across the soft, plush carpet to her door. I swung it open to have the noise come at me in a louder volume, accompanied by a radio announcer speaking over a 70's tune. I briefly turned around to see Jamie still untouched by the racket. Closing the door behind me I made my way, still sleepy, downstairs and towards the noise which was emitting from the kitchen.

As I came closer my pace slowed. At first I wanted to see the cause of all the confusion, but now as I was so close to getting answers I became cautious. I had no idea what was hidden behind that door. It could have been anything, what on earth would be capable of making that ruckus?

I was never really prepared for what was on the other side of the door, but I sure as hell wasn't expecting what I saw.

"Aaahhhh!" I still don't know why I screamed at first.

I mean the sight wasn't all that terrifying. Ok in all fairness it wasn't terrifying at all, but still I think I would have screamed no matter what I saw.

What I met was a wild blur of red, Mrs. Austin. She was swaying left to right in tune with the 70's music that drifted out of the radio sitting by the window while flipping what looked to be an omelet in a pan. Suddenly I became aware of the all too inviting aroma of a hearty breakfast.

She turned around her face contorted in surprise at my outburst. The spatula held in her right hand, frying pan in the other, along with the way she was standing, mid-groove, her butt stuck out a little was enough to make me laugh, but being polite I hid it with a smile.

"Oh, good morning Brooklynn. Sorry honey, did I wake you? I forgot we had company over," she apologized as she turned down the volume on the radio.

"Sorry for screaming, I was just . . . surprised," and I was, the last thing I was expecting to find was Jamie's mom cooking up a storm, listening to music from over thirty years ago, "Whatever you're cooking smells great by the way."

"Thank you dear, come and sit, I was preparing breakfast before I leave. I've got work in an hour," she explained as I took a seat at the round table near the semi circle window.

The table was already set with food. Sausages, eggs, pancakes, and fruits were all laid out in separate platters. My mouth began watering as I looked at all the food. But before I could dig in I remembered my manners and decided to wait until Jamie and her mom were seated also.

I took the time while I was waiting to admire their kitchen. It was cozy and homey; a place that I could imagine held a lot of warm family memories. The appliances were modern giving a contemporary feel yet there were little knickknacks placed sparingly along shelves and atop cupboards.

The rest of the Austin house followed the cozy theme the kitchen held. Jamie and her mom are the only ones who lived there—her parents were divorced. It was a decent sized two storey house with more than enough space for the both of them. Jamie basically had the whole of upstairs to herself. The whole atmosphere was warm and inviting. It was a lot more than I could say for my own home.

Cutting my musings short Jamie entered looking well rested and I wondered how she had been able to sleep through her mom's symphony.

She greeted her mom and came to sit at the table opposite me.

"Do you sleep with earplugs or something?" I asked as I began dishing food onto my plate as they had both joined me at the table.

"No, I've just gotten used to it, sorry I forgot to warn you last night," she smiled as she too placed food onto her plate.

Before I could lift my fork Mrs. Austin spoke up, "Jamie, can you say grace please?" she asked looking at her daughter.

I couldn't help but smile as we bowed our heads to pray. I was used to praying in my mind since I normally ate alone, my mother and I had never sat down to a meal before. It warmed my heart to see how great a family Jamie and her mom was.

Mrs. Austin left around eight not bothering to ask about our departure to school. This I found weird since I knew Jamie hadn't told her mom we'd be skipping.

"She trusts us," she explained when I had asked her.

Her mom was a free spirited soul, I could tell, but I knew she didn't mix matters either. Not bothering to question further I followed Jamie into the living room where she flicked on the T.V.

~~~~~~~~~~~~~~~~~~~

"Well it wasn't the approach I'd take, but ok," she sighed.

"What else am I supposed to do?" I wanted to know.

"Confront his ass! Do something, don't just sit there and pretend nothing happened!" she exclaimed throwing her arms up.

As expected the topic of last night's adventures couldn't be held off for long. After watching an early morning cartoon, the television remained forgotten as we began a conversation. I was opting for the easier way out, avoiding him and living life like I did before. Apparently that wasn't acceptable for Jamie. In her eyes I had the right to verbally abuse him, call him out on his actions. I was supposed to fight back, but I know that wasn't what I would do.

I exhaled deeply leaning back against the couch. I was beyond appreciative of her concern for me, but maybe she was taking this a little harder than necessary. Sure I wanted some sort of revenge on him, make him feel the hurt he had caused, but I wouldn't actually act on it. I wouldn't waste my time or energy on someone that had purposely hurt me. It wasn't worth it.

Jamie on the other hand, you would have sworn Ajay had killed her puppy. It was obvious she was angry, pissed even, because in her eyes he had committed an unforgivable crime. What I didn't understand was why she felt so impacted by something that he did to me. It made me question whether or not their relationship did end on a friendly note as she had stated.

I turned to face her slightly a new thought brewing, "Jamie, why are you taking this so hard?"

She turned to me her face still in amusement from the antics of Tom and Jerry. Only when my question registered her expression turned into slight confusion and shock.

"The whole Ajay thing," I added.

"You're my best friend," she answered like it was obvious that was the reason.

Upon seeing the blank look upon my face she continued, "And it's not right for him to hurt you like that. I'm just looking out for you."

"I know, but it seems that it's something deeper, like he did something to you, something else that's fueling all this anger." I stayed silent after I told her that afraid of her reaction.

She was silent also for a few moments while it looked like she was pondering my statement.

Then she sighed, I thought maybe I said something I shouldn't have and was about to apologize for whatever it was when she spoke, "That's true."

My eyebrows arched a little in surprise at her answer.

"You remember when I told you we had sex . . . well I wasn't a willing participant," she told me.

I gasped in shock and horror, the thought of Ajay forcing her to sexual intercourse was shocking to say the least. From what I had known, from my time with him, he was a very sexual guy, but I couldn't fathom that he would rape her. He was too much of a moral person to violate a woman in such a way.

Her eyes widened at me and she waved her hands frantically shaking her head, "No, no . . . he didn't rape me! Let me rephrase that sentence. I *was* willing, but I was *drunk* . . . I mean *we* were drunk. We weren't in our right minds. We went to a party and had a little too much to drink, I remember stumbling up the stairs and next thing I know I'm waking up next to a fully naked Ajay lying next to me just as naked as I was," she paused remembering the incident.

"I began to freak, it was my first time and I didn't remember using any protection, he woke up and we were both scared shitless. We agreed that it was a mistake, that we shouldn't have done what we had. Then two weeks later I noticed my period was a week late. When I took the pregnancy test I knew I was pregnant."

I nodded my head feeling sympathy for her, "That's why you didn't want to tell him," I now knew why she was so hesitant to tell him.

"Yeah, I mean we were no longer in a relationship, I didn't know how he'd react to being a father and I was so scared," she said.

I remembered the conversation I had eavesdropped on last night, and I remembered Ajay's words . . . *"It's my child too, how long did you plan on hiding that from me, Jamie? When were you going to let me know you were pregnant?"*

It sounded like he cared. But I couldn't really tell.

"What did he say when you told him?" I asked.

She smiled softly, "Nothing, he just looked at me then at my stomach, he kneeled down and put his ear to my belly."

I couldn't help but smile too as a picture materialized in my mind with Ajay listening for his baby's kicks. It was . . . painfully sweet.

I shook my head to get rid of any traces of him and continued listening to her, "I guess that was what I was expecting, wait, no, I wasn't expecting that at all.

"I thought that when he found out he'd be livid and angry or something," she said, not that I would tell her, but I couldn't bring myself to see Ajay getting irate over the fact that he was having a child.

In fact it was quite the opposite; I could easily see him being excited at the thought of being a father. For a moment I felt that I knew him better than she did, better than anyone else did, but I caught myself and continued to listen to Jamie.

"He's not as bad as I thought, but he's an utter ass for hurting you!" Jamie exclaimed.

I couldn't help but laugh a little at her expression. Since she was pregnant, her emotions were kicked up a few notches; at least that's what I guessed. If she got annoyed then she was supper annoyed. If she got angry then she was like a madwoman.

I couldn't help but wonder, if she was always like this, even before the pregnancy. It would be very plausible. Her fiery attitude clashed well with her just as fiery hair. I was beginning to think that pregnancy had nothing to do with her getting so riled up, that maybe she was always just an excited spirit.

Not sure how, but the topic of last night ceased to continue and we settled with watching television for the rest of the morning. It would have been the rest of the morning if Jamie's stomach hadn't growled in hunger causing both of us to divert our attention to her slightly round tummy.

"I think little Jamie is hungry," I chuckled as she rolled her eyes.

"Little Jamie is always hungry," she muttered as she reluctantly got up.

I followed her to the kitchen because I knew that she couldn't cook to save her or her baby's life. She sat at a barstool while I prepared pasta for her.

"It's almost eleven, what on earth are we supposed to do for the remainder of the day?" she asked, chin propped up in her palms.

"I don't know," I mused as I stirred the sauce counter clockwise.

"That smells so good," she leaned over the bar towards the kitchen with her eyes closed, breathing in the aroma of the cooking food.

I looked over my shoulder to laugh at her, "Thanks, and I am pretty sure that's not little 'J' talking."

She giggled before she answered, "Of course not. I haven't had real food in a while."

I laughed as I thought of all the health foods that she had been forced by her mom to eat. I couldn't recall not seeing her with fruit or yogurt. I couldn't blame her for wanting a break. I checked the noodles to make sure they were alright, and as I lowered the lid over the pot a sudden image of Ajay and burnt dinner popped into my mind. I blinked rapidly, surprised at the random memory.

I turned around, leaning against the side of the stove to watch Jamie who was sitting with a bored expression on her face.

"I know we decided to stay home and all, but at the moment, school is looking a lot more fun," she sighed, staring out the window.

"We'll think of something to do, first of all, you need to feed my nephew," I told her scooping a generous helping onto her plate.

I hope she has a boy.

Why?

I've always wanted a little brother.

I grabbed a fork from a side drawer and placed the food on the counter in front of her. With a grateful smile on her face she asked, "What will I ever do without you Brooklynn? You are the best friend anyone could ask for," she picked up her fork, blessed her food and started scooping the sauce laden spaghetti into her mouth.

I walked over to her fridge and opened the door to see it stacked shelf upon shelf with fruits, veggies, yogurts and foreign looking nutrition bars. With a quirked eyebrow I turned to stare at Jamie.

"Where does your mom keep her food?" I asked looking back at all the nourishing foods I would bet were all for the red head devouring her food behind me.

"That is her food," she answered around a mouthful of meatballs.

"What?" I asked not quite believing that Ms. Austin willingly gave up real food to eat the nutrient packed, tasteless stuff that was occupying their fridge.

"She feels bad that I am the only one who has to eat smartly so she decided to eat it with me," she explained through a mouthful of spaghetti.

I smiled at the thought that Mrs. Austin loved her daughter so much as to go to such lengths for Jamie and her baby.

"That's sweet," I mumbled pushing aside everything looking to see if it had anything to drink in there.

I moved to the top shelf and behind some low fat cheese were a box of orange juice and a container of soy milk. I pulled them out and motioned for her to choose one.

"Orange juice please," she politely chose with the fork in her mouth.

I nodded as I placed the soy milk back into its place resting the box on the counter. I glanced around for a few moments as I looked for the cupboard supposedly holding the glassware. I opened the door and took a couple glasses out and put them on the counter near the box of juice. When we were done we still hadn't come up with a genius plan to have fun. It was close to twelve and the metaphorical light bulb that all the cartoons seemed to have hadn't appeared yet.

Needless to say, Jamie and I spent the rest of our school-free Monday afternoon at home with nothing better to do than watch television and lazing around dreading the following day.

November 21—Tuesday

It would have taken us around twenty minutes to reach to school if I hadn't insisted we walk. On top of that I had to swing by my house to get some clothes since Jamie's wouldn't fit right.

The bell had rung approximately five minutes prior to our arrival and I reached my class right as the late bell sounded. As much as I was trying to avoid Ajay I wasn't going to let it affect my perfect punctuality. Being late wasn't on my agenda.

"Take your seats," Mrs. Wyndam drawled out.

I slipped into my seat unnoticed and homeroom went on as usual. In fact the rest of the morning went by quite smoothly without any interruptions, but then it was lunchtime and I had nowhere to hide.

Keeping my head low, eyes on the ground, I made my way through the throng of rushing bodies to the fire escape where I would meet up with Jamie under our rendezvous bleachers.

"Brooklynn!" a voice I was hoping I would not have to hear sounded out over the loud murmur of hungry teenagers.

My pace picked up and I began pushing my way through the crowd at a more vigorous haste.

I made it very far when a hand clamped around my elbow firmly preventing me from going any farther.

"I need to talk to you," he said.

I tugged my arm trying to get it free, but his grip was strong, "No you don't," I muttered loud enough for him to hear trying again to get my arm free.

"Just listen to me, please," he pleaded.

You know how in the movies the girls get all weak-willed and give in to the guy's pleading after he's done them wrong just by the bat of an eyelash?

This was quite the opposite, his pleading wasn't doing me in; it was pissing me off. He had a lot of nerve coming up to me, expecting me to even listen to him after what he did. I didn't care for what he had to say. I didn't want to forgive him.

"No."

With a final tug and a firm glare that hopefully showed him I was serious, I pulled my arm free and continued walking down the hallway.

Is that how he got all the girls he hurt to forgive him? Just by batting a pretty eyelash?

As I walked away I couldn't help but wonder how many girls he actually had hurt before and if I was just another nobody to him. I didn't want to admit it, but the thought of that stung. After all we had done together . . . but come to think of it, it was only six or so days ago. All in six days we went to dinner, he saved me from a potential rape scene, sexually harassed me in my own home . . . twice, saw more of me, emotionally, than anyone ever has (and vice versa) and he hurt me like I hoped he wouldn't.

That's a lot for one week. The most action I had ever had in my life really.

November 22—Wednesday.

I slept over at Jamie's again last night, and I am pretty sure this might become routine for us. Not that I am complaining though, Jamie and Tammy—Mrs. Austin insisted that I call her by her first name—made me feel like part of the family. Something my own mother never bothered to do.

There weren't many classes today since the school was putting on yet another musical production and the first rehearsal was today, they were running a little behind schedule so the rehearsal time was set during school hours since they only had two weeks to get it right. When our teachers began noticing that half the class was away at rehearsals they saw no sense in teaching so for most of the day I had nothing academic to do.

Sometime around fourth period there was a knock at the classroom door, though it was barely audible because of the loud chatter in class. The teacher got up stuck her head outside to talk to the person, probably the principal, then turned around and called my name.

Not at all expecting her to motion for me, I sat there for a few seconds before it registered. I stood and went up to her in confusion as to why she was calling me. Though any misunderstandings I had vanished as I came to the door she was positioned at. Leaning against the door frame, hands in his front pockets, stood Ajay, waiting in all his arrogance.

I rolled my eyes as soon as the teacher closed the door behind me and turned to walk up the hallway. As expected he fell in step beside me.

"You can't keep running from me forever," he said.

I resisted the urge to roll my eyes again, as I ignored him.

I can try

I turned suddenly down a hallway on my right and so did he never missing a step. It was silent except for the sound of our padding footsteps until he realized where I was headed.

Before I could move to push open the door, his hand shot out and grabbed mine. Ripping my hand from his grasp, I tried again but his arm had already beaten me to it. His palm was pressed firmly against the door preventing me from opening it. The girls' bathroom was the only place

I could get away from him for a few minutes and now it wasn't even an option anymore.

I was really frustrated as I spun around, regretting it as I did. I was suddenly caged in by his arm and the wall of the alcove. I instinctively backed up against the door, trying to regain some pace between us.

"Stop running from me, Brooklynn," he firmly said.

"Stop chasing me," I fired back.

"I wouldn't have to be if you would stop running," he replied, "besides you're hurting my feelings."

Psht!

I rolled my eyes at his teasing tone, "Like you hurt mine?"

His playful smirk dropped and his eyes went serious, "If you would just listen to what I have to say . . ."

"I've heard enough," I replied bitterly.

"You haven't heard anything."

"I heard what Jamie said . . ."

"That wasn't true!"

"Of course it was, I just can't believe I didn't see it all along, I mean why else would you even talk to me?"

"Brooklynn-" he started, but I cut him off.

"Then there was the science project, I guess that just tied in greatly with your plan, though I don't understand why you brought me to the party, was it pity? Did you feel sorry for the girl with no life?" I asked cynically.

"You know that's not true," he replied softly.

"Do I? What other reason would there be anyway? I'm the girl no one bothers with, so why did you? Obviously it was to use me to get information on Jamie, I just feel really stupid now because I let myself believe that for once I was actually worth another person's while."

I didn't mean for all of that to slip out, but it did and I didn't want to hear him make fun of me for being so pathetic. I kept my gaze downward never looking him in the eyes and slipped out from under his arm and back down the hallway.

I kept walking until my feet became blurry, not realizing that I was involuntarily crying. I wiped vigorously at my eyes, inwardly berating myself for getting so emotional. Making sure that all my tears were gone I continued on my way back to class, but only went a few steps when the bell for lunch rang.

I sighed tiredly as I switched my direction to the fire escape route that I had become so accustomed to in the past week.

"How was your-what happened?" Jamie asked as she saw my face.

I was sure there weren't any signs of tears on my cheeks or anything so it was a bit unexpected that she asked that.

"I can see it in your eyes, so tell me what happened or who hurt you so I can go punch in their face."

I quirked my eyebrow at her 5'4 frame skeptically. I doubt she'd be a match in a fight with Ajay.

"Ajay, just cornered me and tried to apologize, but I went blurting out things like a madwoman and ran away," I summarized the scenario for her as I took my seat.

She was silent for a few moments before she answered, "He tried to apologize?"

I nodded and she seemed to be a bit surprised that Ajay would attempt to apologize to anyone.

"He must be really sorry," she mused aloud, "but that still doesn't change what he did."

I nodded indifferently not wanting to care about it either way. I sat down besides her engaging in conversation, an attempt to stray away from speaking of Ajay. I didn't entirely accomplish that task as we started a conversation about father figures in our lives. I had told her the story behind mine, but all I knew about hers was that he lived somewhere in Wisconsin because he and her mother divorced when she was seven.

Apparently she hadn't seen him in six years, last time being when she was ten years old.

"He has a new family now, a wife and twin girls," she said smiling lightly but I saw the hurt clearly in her eyes.

"Don't you miss him?" I asked knowing she would tell me the truth.

"Yeah, a little, I mean I sort of miss the stuff we used to do, we weren't all that close or anything, but it hurts to know that he moved on and had two kids with another woman, at first it made me feel that I was inadequate for him," she said not bothering to hide the pain with a smile.

I realized that Jamie was a lot like me in that area of life, I could relate to her easily, although I had never known my dad, I did wish sometimes that I had a father to look up to. I always envied the other kids going on camping trips with their dad and I often wondered what I was missing out.

But most of all, it hurt to know that my dad didn't even know I existed, and I doubted he cared either. I didn't even know what he looked like, was he still alive? What kind of person was he? Have I ever encountered him not knowing the man before me was my father?

Sometime when I was in elementary school, I had this strong desire to know who my father was. I was always speculating any man that resembled me in some way. If he had big brown eyes, dark hair, or high cheek bones my head would start swirling with the possibilities of him being the man who impregnated my mother sixteen years ago.

"How come you haven't seen him in over five years?" I asked not understanding the wide time gap between their meetings with one another.

"Well after the first two years after the divorce he stopped calling to speak to me, didn't visit as much and never asked me to come over anymore, then before I knew what was happening, my mom told me that he had gotten remarried two years back.

"It hit me kind of hard to hear that, he didn't even call to tell me," there was a bitter tone in her voice as she said this.

I couldn't blame her, I was bitter in my own situation as well.

"Anyway, that's my story," she said after a minute of silence had dawned between us.

I looked up as soon as the lunch bell rang signaling the end of lunch hour, cutting off any reply I was about to give.

We stood up from our comfortable spot and reluctantly made our way back to class.

By the time school was officially dismissed for the day I had already been down the hallway, ready to meet Jamie near the front stairs so we could head home.

Outside, the air was crisp and cool even though it was well into the afternoon, this due to the nearing winter season.

I hadn't been waiting long enough for Jamie to make it from her class on the opposite side of the building when a hand rested on my shoulder. I turned around ready to tell Ajay to save his breath when I was met with the face of Dakota Richards grinning down at me.

"Hey," he greeted me the grin still ghosting his features.

My frown must have given him an indication to my confusion.

"Oh I'm waiting here for Jamie, we have a project to do together," he explained.

"Ok," I said not having anything else to respond.

"Have you finished your project yet?" he inquired a few seconds later.

"Not yet," I answered briefly wondering why he felt the need to make small talk with me.

"Is it because of the whole thing with Ajay?" he quizzed.

What the heck do you think?!

I was a bit taken aback by his forward question.

"We're best friends, I'd figure out at some point in time," he smiled casually answering my internal query.

I nodded my head, I should have known he would know, Tristan obviously knew too since he was in the room with Ajay and Jamie the night of the party.

"You know, Ajay being an asshole shouldn't have to affect your grades, I mean you could always ask Mr. Dennis to switch partners or even join another group or something," he stated calmly with a small smile.

I was shocked that he hadn't supported Ajay in the matter and didn't seem to be biased at all. It was nothing I was expecting from his best friend. My eyebrows involuntarily lifted at his blunt remark.

"Just because I am his best friend does not mean I think he is always right, I believe he messed up and he deserves the treatment you're dishing out."

I just stood wordlessly as I heard him criticize his best friend shamelessly. Suddenly I viewed Dakota in a new light. I respected him more for his honesty and perception of things.

Not because he appeared to agree with me, but because he didn't feel strained to abide by the wrong his friend had done.

"Thanks," I responded just as Jamie made her way downstairs towards us.

"Hey guys, ready to go?" she asked adjusting the strap of her bag on her shoulder.

Dakota played the role of understanding older brother very well and I was beginning to think he was the big brother that I never had.

It was sometime near four o clock and in the middle of their research for their topic of physiology. It had been relatively quiet with the odd murmur or laugh at every interval. Dakota's phone rang, he excused himself, getting up and moving away from us.

I took that as my cue to talk to Jamie, "You two make such a cute couple," I said softly, still at risk of him hearing me.

She blushed, rolling her eyes, but I knew she was happy for the comment. It was true; it was also obvious how much they liked each other. Every time he wasn't looking she would steal a glance and vice versa. I had been noticing this for the past hour and a half. Then when their hands accidentally bumped a light blush would crawl up both of their faces.

"You think so?" she asked, apparently they were both oblivious to the obvious attraction between them.

"Of course, he's been watching you out of the corner of his eye the whole time and so have you, don't think I don't know," I said grinning when her cheeks reddened.

"Do you think he . . ."

She cut off as both of our ears picked up on Dakota talking in the kitchen.

"She's not going to talk to you, man," he said.

There was a silence as Jamie and I looked at each other with the same curious/suspicious glance.

"I know you didn't intend to, but I doubt she wants to listen to you explain anything right now," silence . . ."I'll try but I doubt it'll work."

"At Jamie's, doing a project," silence . . ."Yeah, she's here, but I don't think that's a good idea."

"Listen Ajay, I got to go, don't do anything stupid, yes, that's something stupid. I'll talk to you later man, bye."

What was that all about?

Before I could get an answer we heard Dakota making his way back into the living room so Jamie and I began talking like we had been in a conversation the entire time and not eavesdropping like we had been.

"She tried to, but it didn't work," I blurted out the first words that formed a coherent sentence in my mind.

"Well maybe she didn't try hard enough, I mean how stupid could a person be?" Jamie answered and for a second I didn't know how to respond, but I added something anyway.

"It's not her fault really; I mean how could she have known on such short notice?" I countered.

"Brooklynn, she knew three days in advance, I am pretty sure that was enough time."

"To hack into a school network sure, but to infiltrate Wal-Mart's whole system, now that's tough," I strung out surprising myself at the turn the conversation was taking.

"Ok well when you put it like that, I guess it makes sense that she failed, but still, wasn't she like the number one person in her field?" Jamie quizzed.

"I doubt Wal-Mart's a piece of cake to hack into," Dakota had come back into the room already, but we had gotten so engaged in our improvised conversation we paid him little heed. Besides this was turning out to be lots of fun, who knew?

She paused a moment and so did I actually wondering about the truth of my statement. The moment though was short lived when Dakota decided to speak.

"Um, do I want to know?" he asked.

We just smiled at him knowing that he really didn't want to.

Sitting back, project totally forgotten we engaged in light conversation. I sat back on my palms turned down on the soft carpet and watched as Jamie and Dakota exchanged words completely ignoring the fact that I was right there, not like it mattered to me, it was fun to watch Jamie blush every time he directed a question at her. And since he was only talking to her, her cheeks held a lasting pink tinge. When it started to get a little uncomfortable for me having to watch them flirt, I decided it was my cue to make an exit.

"Hey Jamie, I better head home to get my stuff," I said looking for an excuse to give them time alone.

She looked up, "Um, oh ok, sure," she said trying to hide the fact that she was staring at him again.

I smiled as I stood up, grabbing my sweater from her sofa and slipped it on while making my way to the small entrance hall where I'd let myself out.

"Bye guys," I bid them right as I slipped out the front door.

I turned to head down the path, but then spun in a 180 degree turn ready to go back inside.

"Brooklynn wait!"

I sighed with my hand on the doorknob, ready to go back inside, but then I remembered Jamie and Dakota. They needed this time alone and I didn't want to take away from that.

I turned around to come face to face with a slightly panting Ajay.

"You have no reason to me angry with me," he stated before I could ask him what he wanted.

"Excuse me?" I asked bewildered that he thought I had no cause to be angry with him.

Is he serious? Of course I have every reason to be angry!

"You're angry because you think I used you," he stated.

Duh!

I rolled my eyes at his obvious statement, titling my head to the side waiting for him to continue.

"But I didn't, so you have no right to be angry," he continued.

"What do you mean, you didn't? Why else would you even think about befriending me?" I asked.

"Maybe I thought that you were a sweet girl, maybe I wanted to get to know you better," he said, "ever think about that being a possibility?"

I just folded my arms having nothing to say to his question. Seeing my apparent rebuttal in my stance he went on.

"Why is it that you think I would intentionally hurt you?" he asked softly.

"You can't tell me that you didn't want to ask what was happening with Jamie," I accused not comfortable with forgiving him just yet.

"Sure I was curious, but that doesn't mean that's why I talked to you. I wanted to get to know you," he said looking me straight in the eye.

"Why didn't you deny it when she accused you of using me at the party then, you hesitated," I asked wanting to know why he had hesitated to deny the accusation that night.

He smiled lightly, "I just found out that I was gonna be a father, sorry for not being in my right state of mind," he said.

I sighed in resignation. I guess it all made sense and maybe I was too hard on him for blaming him without even giving him a fair chance, but that's how I was. I expected him to hurt me the moment I began to trust him. It was my nature. It seemed natural that he would have done something to upset me. It's just the way I think, in all fairness to me.

Besides it was taking up a lot of energy to be constantly angry with him.

"So . . . am I forgiven?" he asked with hopeful eyes as he looked at me.

I hesitated a moment deciding it wouldn't hurt if I forgave him. I nodded and his face broke into a small smile. A questioning look came into his eyes as he looked at me, but I didn't know what he wanted.

I looked down and I saw his arms spread open as if he was gesturing towards me. Then it dawned that he was asking permission for a hug. I raised my eyebrows in slight surprise but I stepped closer to him and gave him a hug anyway. His arms were one of the few places I was comfortable in. A reassuring sense of security and protection cascaded over me when I was in his embrace. We pulled away and an awkward silence fell. This was the part that no one liked, the discomfited part right after a reconciliation that occurs after a fight.

Breaking the silence, "where are you headed?" he asked.

"Home, actually," I answered gesturing that I was heading down the pathway.

He moved aside and we walked down the lane side by side.

When we reached my front door we still hadn't said much to each other, but I invited him inside anyway as it seemed like the natural thing to do.

I shrugged off my sweater and placed it as well as his in the coat closet, sighing when the warmth of the central heating greeted me. Winter was near and the seasonal change was bitingly cold as expected.

"We still have that project to do," I said as he followed me into the kitchen.

"You had to remind me?" he asked.

I smiled at his delinquent attitude towards our science project, "want anything to eat or drink?" I asked.

"No thanks, I'm fine," he said as he took a seat at the bar.

I leaned back on the island's counter and we just let silence consume us as we stared at each other.

"I feel like things aren't back to how they were," he mused aloud.

I responded with a small sigh, "It might take a while for it to return to normal." I mean I forgave him, but I wasn't so willing to trust him again, even though he did nothing wrong as proven, it's just the way I work. It takes a lot for me to trust someone. And though it wasn't really his fault, he lost it.

"How long is a while?" he asked leaning forward to rest his elbows on the bar countertop.

"I don't know, however long it takes for us to be comfortable with each other again," I stated.

"Hm, can we go to your room?" he asked.

I let out a laugh, "I was sort of waiting for that, knowing you have a thing for hanging out in my room," I said pushing off the counter and making my way upstairs.

"I don't have a thing for it . . . I just feel a lot more comfortable there," he said.

It occurred to me that my bedroom was a familiar place for him. Not *my* room exclusively, but a girl's room in general. It was no secret that Ajay was a hit with females. It was common territory for him. Like natural habitat, of course that's where he felt most comfortable when he came over. Not saying that he was thinking along the same lines as he did when he was at one of his conquest's house, no, we were only friends. But it made sense why he felt so snug in my room. It was just a thought that popped into mind as we ascended the stairs.

It was sort of like we had picked up where we left off when we took our places on my bed and divulged in conversation.

"Tristan said to say hi," he told me as I was playing with a loose thread on one of my pillows.

I looked up in slight puzzlement, "uh ok," I replied.

"He's a really friendly guy, he saw you at the party and never got a chance to introduce himself, and he feels bad about it," he explained.

I nodded my head never thinking of dubbing Tristan as one of those sociable and open people. Yeah I know it was stereotyping, but it's the way he dressed and looked. They all were defying what I originally thought of them. The dark clothing and angst styled hair were just styles.

"You know thinking of it; you and your friends are totally different. I don't know either of you so well, but from what I can tell, all of you contrast in some way," I said.

"You mean Dakota, Tristan and I?" he asked.

"Yeah, the three of you are like strawberry, chocolate and vanilla ice cream. You know, three totally different flavors, but go well together," I told him.

"I guess we make a good team," he simply replied, "have you ever talked to Tristan or Dakota?"

"I've never talked to Tristan but I was with Dakota today at Jamie's and he is really sweet. Like the big brother type," I said remembering my afternoon with the two lovebirds.

He was silent before he spoke then something seemed to click, "oh yeah when I called he said something about you being there."

I smiled remembering how Jamie and I had eavesdropped and then made up a spurious story about a hacker and Wal-Mart.

"You and Jamie are sort of different too," he said.

I nodded my head knowing what he meant. We were almost complete opposites. But it worked well in the sense that we weren't in danger of stepping on each other's toes and we sort of brought out each other . . . in each other, if that makes sense.

"Yeah, her hair isn't just a prop," I said thinking how her personality matched her untamed and fiery red hair.

It was silent for a moment as I thought about asking him something and wondering if it wasn't too personal. Deciding I wanted to know I went ahead, "sorry if this is too personal but, what are you planning to do now?"

I didn't need to explain further as he already caught what I was implying, hesitating for a moment he answered, "I'm not sure, I mean this is so unexpected, I never thought I'd be a father, at least not so soon."

I nodded at his reply. It must be tough for him; Jamie had gotten over the initial shock and was now very accepting of the fact that she had conceived a child, besides she had her mother there for support. Now when I was on the other half of the matter I realized maybe Ajay wouldn't take it the way Jamie had.

"Are you ready for a baby?" I asked.

He smiled lightly with a distant look in his emerald green eyes as he replied, "I'm not ready to be a dad, but I'm willing to try. I don't know how either, but I am willing to learn."

I smiled at his response, it was so obvious that he would do anything for his child; it was evident in his eyes as he talked. I admired that about him, the fact that he didn't cast away the matter by not taking responsibility for his actions and his baby. It wasn't a trait one could find in many adolescent boys of today.

"Are you ready for a baby," I was caught off guard by that question.

Catching my expression he added quickly, "There was no insinuation in that question. I just wanted to know if it happened, if you'd be ready."

I waited a moment or two contemplating whether I would be ready for one or not. I never really thought about it before, having one now nor having one later. It just never crossed my mind. Would I be ready for one now? I doubt it. I was still going to school; I was certain I'd get no help from my 'loving' mother so how was I supposed to take care of it when I didn't know anything about parenting? Did I even want a baby? Whether now or later on in life I was not positive. I didn't want one now that was certain, but did I ever want to have children?

Now that gives me a lot to think about.

"Not now," I answered simply.

He nodded his head and leant back on my bed getting comfortable. I began watching his face since his eyes were closed and he couldn't see me staring. His facial bone structure was defined, a lot like a male model's which made me wonder if he did model part time or something. His expression was peaceful and at rest and when it wasn't smirking at me, it was boyish and looked almost innocent. Almost, because even when he was resting I could tell he had experienced a lot, been though some weathered times. His face contained maturity. My gaze slid from his face to linger on the rest of his body. It was lean and built with ample muscle; his arms were strong I noticed, they weren't ripped and defined in a bodybuilder way, but it was obvious he worked out.

I had never actually gotten to see his abdomen so I don't have a description for that, but I could tell it was firm and toned form the three hugs we shared. So I guessed if he didn't have a six pack, he was still appreciatively toned.

"It's rude to stare," I snapped my head to his face as I heard his voice.

His jade green eyes were now open and twinkling with mischief.

"Sorry," I mumbled turning away, a slight blush rising to my cheeks at the fact that he had caught me staring.

"It's okay, just as long as I get to return the favor," he said smirking.

I smiled lightly and rolled my eyes at his Ajay-like ways.

He chuckled and sat up, "You know I missed hanging out with you, in the past two days," he stated.

I quirked my eyebrow at him, "Is *the* Ajay Edison going soft on me?" I questioned with a soft chuckle.

"Never, just realizing how much he missed a friend," he said looking intently at me with his mesmerizing emerald eyes.

I wasn't sure how to respond to that, but right on time the signal for an instant message sounded and my head turned to see that someone had in fact sent me an IM. I slipped off my bed well aware that Ajay's eyes had never left me; apparently he was 'returning the favor'. I clicked on the blinking bar at the bottom of the screen and a window appeared.

Jamie had sent a message, which was surprising in itself because I had thought she would have been too busy with Dakota to bother to be online and send me a message.

Ringmaster93 says: *When are you coming back?*

New York says: *That depends, is Dakota still there?*

Ringmaster93 says: *Yeah, why??*

New York says: *Well I wouldn't wanna interrupt anything between you two*

I laughed softly as I pictured her face turning red in a bashful blush.

Ringmaster93 says: *You wouldn't be, but thanks; I'll call you when we're done kay?*

New York says: *Sure, take your time.*

Ringmaster93 has signed off

I smiled shaking my head, for a girl that had been through more than the average teen-aged girl she was still so very innocent.

I joined Ajay back on the bed and his eyes were closed again, I doubted he was sleeping though; I was still cautious because of a few minutes ago when he surprised me.

I noticed his silence was something I wasn't used to, so, I decided to question him about it, "Long day?" I asked.

His eyes didn't open as he answered, "Sort of," he stated briefly.

"What made it so long?" I asked shifting my position on the bed.

"Well, running after you and trying to beg for your forgiveness is a job all on its own, and as if that wasn't enough I have some overdue bills to pay," he said.

Realization dawned as I remembered Ajay lived on his own. I never considered that he had the responsibility of owning a house. Paying bills, mortgage and taxes, he must be really stressed. Suddenly, I saw him in a whole new light. He was only eighteen, in his last year of high school, orphaned and left with the responsibilities of taking care of his house, paying bills and getting an education.

There was a short silence since I wasn't sure what to say. I wanted to ask about his parents and his situation of being orphaned but then I thought that maybe that might be too personal and out of place to ask.

"Ajay, can I ask you a question?" I asked, knowing that I already did in asking to ask . . .

He nodded his head, eyes still closed so I took that as my ok to go ahead, "How long ago?"

"About five years ago," he said not bothering to clarify my query since he knew what I was asking.

That meant he was thirteen at the time, which brought me to another bout of questions. Where did he go? Either he lived at an orphanage or a relative's house, but before I could get the chance to ask him any of this he spoke.

"I lived with my uncle after they died; he took care of me and when I turned eighteen about a week ago, I moved back into my old house, where my parents and I lived before they were killed."

My eyes widened as he finished. Killed? They were killed, I had no idea. He didn't see my expression because his eyes were still shut. A wave of sympathy washed over me for this boy, the things he'd been put through, I'd had no idea.

"Killed?" I whispered not sure how the question would affect him.

"Yeah, an upset employee snapped and began firing rounds in the building, killing over twenty people including my parents. Then he turned and shot himself with his own gun. Ended up being just one big mess and no one to blame or press charges against. The one day they decided to go into the office was the same day this guy thought he'd take the lives of twenty something unlucky people," I was quiet as I listened to him.

I could feel the pain and hurt in his voice, but when I saw a tear trickle down his temple and disappear into his hair I felt at that moment my heart reach out to him. Silently, I got up on all fours and crawled over to where he was lying down. His eye lids were still closed as I leant down and hugged him. A moment later I felt his arms envelop me in a firm embrace.

As I laid there hugging him I could only imagine the pain he was feeling. Having his both parents murdered at the tender age of thirteen. The only parent I had was my mother and even though she wasn't the best, I don't know how I'd cope without her. She didn't hug me or show any affection, but I knew she loved me despite it all and I loved her too.

My cheek was suddenly wet with his tears and I tightened my hold about him. I had to shut my eyes to prevent myself from letting a few slip as well.

He was so vulnerable in this moment that I just wanted to hold him and wish away his pain and tears. This was a side to him that I had never before seen and I didn't want to see often. It impaired me to witness him like this. The strong, witty, mystifying Ajay I knew had vanished and in his place, laid a broken boy who needed a friend. I would keenly be that friend. I would hug him when he needed one and I would try to give him the love he clearly lost years ago.

I'm not certain how long we lay there, maybe a bit over ten minutes, but we were startled by my phone ringing away on my side table. I lifted myself off of him and went over to my phone, flipping it open and answering when I noticed the caller was none other than Jamie.

"Yes?" I inquired, propping myself up on one hand while I held the phone in my other.

"Am I interrupting something?" she asked.

I rolled my eyes, presently thinking Jamie's perverted thoughts made up for all her innocence.

"No, Jamie, I'm just in an awkward position that's all," I regretted my words as they left my lips knowing the interpretation she was going to get.

"Ooh, really-" I cut her off before she could say anything else.

"It's not what you think woman, get your mind out of the gutter, I'm holding myself up with one hand so I won't fall over," I explained.

"Oh," she sounded slightly disappointed.

I smiled as I thought of how she thought I needed a boyfriend and how she must have had the notion I was with someone, well I was, but not in that sense.

"Anyway, when will you be done?" I asked.

"I am done, I was calling to tell you to come over whenever you're ready," she said.

I shifted my body because my arm was beginning to hurt from the strain of my weight, "Ok, um I'll be there in half an hour, just lemme get my stuff ready."

"Now? What were you doing all this time?" she queried.

"Tell you when I get there," I replied.

"Ok, see ya later."

"Alright, bye," I hung up the phone, tossed it back on the table and fell onto the bed with a huff relieving my arm of the strain.

"Was Jamie always that perverted?" I asked Ajay wondering if she was always that way.

"Yep, you say that like it's a bad thing," he replied.

I raised my head to look at him, "I think you're a bad influence on her," I accused.

"Am not," he defended himself, "she was like that before we even got together."

I thought about Ajay and Jamie in a relationship with their perverted ways, and laughed inwardly, they probably made a perfect couple and I said as much.

"Not really, that was all there was in our relationship, laughter and jokes. I mean it's not bad to have those things in a relationship, but that's all ours was made up of," he said.

I propped up myself on my elbows to look at him, "What do you mean?"

"I mean, a relationship is supposed to be filled with love and understanding, you're supposed to share your secrets and connect with each other on a certain level, all we had was a good time that ended in drunken sex," he said.

I was taken aback by his interpretation of what a relationship is supposed to be and his harsh words about his and Jamie's.

I felt it was unfair for him to say those things about what they shared since I had yet to hear Jaime's point of view on their relationship. I knew she wasn't yearning away after him, but I didn't know how she felt when they were together. I made a mental note to ask her later tonight.

I got off from the bed and went over to my dresser, taking out a few pieces of clothing and placing them in my duffel bag.

"What are you doing?" he asked sitting up.

"Getting my stuff ready, I'm going over to Jamie's in a while," I said stopping to see his reaction.

It now occurred to me that he didn't know and I didn't want to offend him by leaving him to go over to Jamie. He nodded and continued watching so I guessed he was fine with it. I continued putting stuff in my bag when he asked, "How many nights are you staying for?"

"Maybe the rest of the week," I said, "Why?"

"Would it be okay to work at her house for the project? He asked.

I had almost forgotten we still had the practical part of the project to do.

"Um, sure I guess, I don't think she'd mind, Dakota and her are partners anyway so we could all work on our projects," I reasoned as I threw a pair of jeans into the bag.

I went into my bathroom and grabbed my bag of toiletries and tossed that into my bag as well.

"Why are you staying there so long?" he quizzed.

"It gets lonely here sometimes," I briefed as I bent down to zip up my bag.

"Your mom's away on a business trip or something?"

"Or something. She left on Friday, or was it Saturday?" I wondered, not really bothered either way.

I left the bag on the floor and went back to the bed where I sat beside him.

"Aren't you leaving?" he asked when he looked over at me.

Deciding to ignore how rude that statement sounded, "I said I'd be there in half an hour, I now have twenty five minutes left, and it takes way less than that to walk to her house, I think I can relax for a bit," I said looking at him.

He nodded and continued playing with one of my throw pillows. Suddenly a conversation we had before had popped into my mind and I began laughing.

His brow rose in question as he glanced at me.

"I never did get to see you make out with Tristan or Dakota," I mused.

He broke into a small smile, "well you kind of ran off on me on Sunday so I didn't get a chance to show you."

"Well there is always another time," I said indifferently.

"Of course, I know how much you want to see it anyway," he said wriggling his eyebrows playfully.

Rolling my eyes, I responded with, "I don't want to, you convinced me to remember? I just never dubbed you for being bisexual," I said.

"I'm not," he said.

My brows furrowed in confusion and he went on, "We don't make out because we want to, we do it, because girls want us to," he explained.

"Why?" I had yet to see what was so appealing about two guys making out.

"You'll see, soon enough and then you too will be begging me to do it," he smirked.

I rolled my eyes at him, "Why listen to them, what do you get out of it?" I asked.

"Girls think it's hot, which means they think we're hot, c'mon you have to see the reasoning in that," he said grinning.

"Not really, you're already hot so why bother?"

He raised an eyebrow at me and I blushed at my words, "You think I'm hot?"

"The whole school is in love with you, don't act so surprised," I said.

He threw his head back and let out a hearty laugh. I wasn't expecting that, I wasn't expecting that at all so being slightly weirded out, I just sat back and watched as bouts of laughter shook his body. In my moment of selfness I thought about how contrasting it was to see two extremely opposite emotions displayed by him in such a short space of time.

This boy never ceases to amaze me

Sure right about that? Why is he still laughing?

My eyebrows lifted slightly as I watched him fall back onto my bed still laughing crazily. What was so funny about what I had said? I thought I was complimenting him in a way, I didn't think he'd find it *that* amusing. Still, I waited patiently as he calmed down, the laughing not as wild and uncontrolled as before. He sat back up and I was afraid to say anything else in case he thought that would be funny too. When there was only silence I considered saying something, but he beat me to it.

"Sorry, I just thought that was funny," he explained.

"Obviously," I muttered looking at him with a raised eyebrow.

"It reminded me of something Tristan said a while back and it was hilarious, just brought back a few memories," he briefed me further.

Still questioning his sanity I nodded my head and slid off my bed to slip the duffel bag strap over my shoulder.

I turned to him, "Ready to leave now, it's almost six thirty."

I waited as he got off the bed before turning to walk out of my room. Gripping the handrail to go downstairs I paused trying to remember if I had forgotten anything. When nothing came to mind I brushed it off and continued down the stairwell with Ajay a few steps behind.

When I locked the door and began down the pathway I had expected Ajay to go in the other direction not continue on by my side. I paused when I reached the end of my street.

"Um, where are you going?" I hesitated before asking.

"Jamie's, right?" he asked.

I squinted in confusion, "Well, that's where *I'm* going."

"So am I, I'll probably go home with Dakota," he said shoving his hands into his pockets.

I nodded my head and continued on my journey figuring if he wanted to tag along then I couldn't stop him.

When I raised my hand to press the doorbell for the Austin's residence it occurred to me that Ajay and Jamie would be in the same room together since the night of the party. Would there be tension between them? I wasn't sure what to expect. I didn't want to be feeling uncomfortable if they were on sour terms.

Before I could open my mouth to query Ajay about this, the door swung open and my best friend's radiant face answered.

"Great, you're here," she hugged me and pulled me inside.

"Hi Ajay," she addressed him casually and I stiffened as I watched them.

I didn't know what I was expecting to see, but I never thought the air between them would be so not . . . tense. It was as if they were buddies, not ex lovers with a child on the way.

"Hey."

My shoulders relaxed and I let out a soft breath I wasn't aware I was holding. I admired the maturity between them on this whole situation.

"Dakota is in the den playing *Splinter Cell Conviction*," she told him to which he nodded in acknowledgment before going off towards the den.

The look on her face told me she was expecting a full story detail by detail of what happened in the time span I was absent from her house.

"Tonight," I briefly told her and she nodded knowing she would hear it all soon enough.

I followed her into the kitchen where I sat at a bar stool while she went to get us drinks. She pulled out two juice boxes from the fridge and I eyed her as she placed them on the countertop before me.

"What, I like bendy straws and there's no dishes to wash after," she slipped into a seat beside me and punctured the box with the straw.

I followed suit and we began talking, "What happened?" I asked eager to find out what had happened with her and Dakota while I was away.

Her tell-tale blush appeared and I knew something juicy must have occurred. I sat up straighter in my chair ready to listen to the full story.

She looked over her shoulders to see if the boys were coming up from the den and when she heard their cheers of triumph and the game's gruesome sound effects she continued.

"We kissed!" our squeals could be heard throughout the whole of downstairs but we doubted that they heard us over their roar of laughter. There were only two boys in there, you'd think there was a party going on in her den.

"Tell me, how'd it happen?" I asked leaning forward wanting to hear.

"When you left he moved closer to me," I nodded happy that my plan had worked.

"Then when I moved my hand to get the pencil he caught it and held it in his, I could have melted," she sighed, "but then when he pulled me into him and kissed me I practically did melt."

I giggled along with her; it was so cute the way they were around each other. Dakota obviously cared for her and Jamie was head over heels, I could tell. I admired that about them, I wanted someone like that to be there for me. I was almost jealous of the two.

I listened as she told the story. The look in her eyes was far away. I could tell she was still entranced by the events that took place when I left them. I perched my chin in my upturned palm and continued to pay attention to her detailed replay of what had happened when I left.

"So what happened with you and Ajay?" she questioned leaning towards me in eagerness to hear my story.

As soon I was about to let her know of what had happened when I left I was interrupted by the sound of footsteps and laughter coming down the hallway towards the kitchen. I closed my mouth and she gave me a look letting me know she'd be on my case as soon as they left.

"I'm headed home," Dakota announced sitting on a bar stool alongside Jamie.

Ajay stood on the other side of the counter leaning forward to talk to us. I shifted in my seat subtly taking in our positions; it was obvious that Dakota and Jamie were more than just friends. Turning to look at Ajay he looked relaxed in his surrounding, on closer inspection though I still couldn't find any evidence of jealousy or anything that would give me reason to believe that he liked Jamie in anyway.

Shaking my head, I was slightly not sure why I was analyzing Ajay to see if he still felt anything towards Jamie.

After a few minutes of mindless and amicable chatter Dakota stood from his perch alongside his hunny bunny and announced that he was ready to head home. Ajay walked around the counter dividing him from us and came to stand next to me. Jamie and I stood to show them to the door. She swung open the oak front door, but instead of letting them out like I had initially thought she would, she followed Dakota to his car at the end of the walkway. It was a little after sunset but it was still bright enough to see Dakota lean towards Jamie in a much more than friendly manner.

I turned away allowing them their privacy to see Ajay leaning against the wall adjacent to the door with his hands placed in his pockets. The fact that he was staring at me with intense green eyes when I turned around was slightly unnerving. Folding my arms across my chest I countered his gaze with one of my own.

My stare was broken by the faint sound of a giggle coming from outside. I didn't have to turn to know that it was Jamie. Returning my stare to Ajay I realized that I didn't know if he was comfortable with his best friend dating his ex and the mother of his child.

Biting my bottom lip I considered asking him, but wasn't sure if it was the right place or time. Knowing that I might probably forget later on I decided to do it now, "Are you okay with Jamie and Dakota being more than friends?" I asked cautiously.

He quirked an eyebrow as an amused smirk spread across his face, "If they're happy then why wouldn't I be?" he answered with a question.

"Well I thought that maybe it would be awkward for you to see them together after you two were together," I answered.

"I told you already, I have no feelings for Jamie, so it doesn't faze me who she dates, besides we're all grown up here. I think we're mature enough not to do that whole "off limits" thing."

I nodded in understanding realizing that they were mature enough not to follow such preteen guidelines on relationships.

"Besides, I wouldn't expect Jamie to be upset if I started dating you," he said, "If she dates one of my best friends then she should be open to the idea about me dating hers, don't you think?" he asked moving forward to stand in front of me.

Not expecting the conversation to take such an abrupt turn I didn't have an appropriate response. What was I supposed to say anyway? He just implied that it would be okay to date each other. Thankfully, I was used to his antics by now so I wasn't completely shocked by his statement.

"Maybe," I shrugged.

"Oh?" he asked evidently amused.

I nodded as I leaned back into the wall directly behind me.

"What do you mean by 'maybe'?" he asked.

"Well it depends, dating her friend out of spite wouldn't be okay," seeing the look on his face I added, "but since we established that you had no feelings for Jamie then it wouldn't be out of malice.

"Also it depends on if you like that friend,"—I was cut off.

"I do like that friend," he smirked stepping closer.

Finding a sudden bout of courage I responded with, "What if that friend doesn't like you?"

I almost laughed at the expression that his face now held. It was a mixture between confusion and disbelief. Did he really think all girls swooned at the sight of him? He couldn't believe that someone was not attracted to him.

"Why would that friend not like me?" he asked looking me straight in the eyes.

Amused, I answered, "Lots of reasons, you're arrogant, conceited, a player, hardly care for anyone else's feelings most of the time, and the list goes on," I said.

"I am not arrogant or conceited,"—he went on to defend himself, but I cut him off.

"The fact that you're surprised that a girl isn't head over heels for you makes you very much so," I pointed out challenging him to say otherwise.

"I'm used to having girls like me, so what?" he replied.

"That's what I meant about you being a player, how many girlfriends have you ever had?"

117

He hesitated a moment before opening his mouth, but nothing came out except, "I've lost count."

"And that doesn't even include how many flings you've had with random girls, most of whom you left broken hearted or hurt," I stated.

"You make me sound like a bad person," he said sounding defeated.

"You're not a bad person Ajay, just a little untrustworthy," I said softening at the look on his face.

"You don't trust me?" he asked eyes snapping up to locate mine.

"I trust you to a certain extent, but not fully."

"How can I get you to trust me fully?" he asked catching me off guard.

"I don't know. What would it matter?" I asked.

"Because friends trust each other, how are we supposed to be friends if you don't fully trust me?" he asked.

"It'll come with time I guess," I said.

"How long will that be, I don't wanna wait too long," he replied.

"Why do you really want my trust so badly?" I asked with hint of suspicion of him having a hidden agenda.

"Because I care about you and I want you to confide in me. I want to be the one you come crying to and tell your secrets to," he answered still looking at me with his intense gaze.

I faltered a bit. That was so sincere I just couldn't help but believe him. I couldn't help but want to ask out of curiosity and maybe I wanted to know his answer, "Do you trust me?" I asked.

"Yes," he didn't hesitate.

"Why?" I asked, confused, I hadn't done anything to earn much of his trust and I said as much.

"Because you chose to be my friend," he said with a small smile.

"I don't get it," I replied, that didn't mean he had to trust me at all.

He sighed before answering still looking at me with his intensely beautiful green eyes, "you didn't have to let me sleep over those two times, you didn't have to believe me and forgive me today or even comfort me when I was crying after I told you about my parents, but you did. Friends are always there for each other and you were there for me, and I believe you always will be there for me."

I looked down and realized that I had meant a lot to him. He appreciated me, which was a feeling I've only felt with Jamie. Him appreciating me made me appreciate him even more.

I walked forward and enveloped him in a firm embrace. In a way I was responding to him, I was saying I would always be there for him. His arms came about my torso as he returned it not a moment later.

Man, I love his hugs

I wonder why?

Shut up . . . because they are reassuring.

Our hug was cut short as Dakota's car horn sounded impatiently. We pulled away to realize that Jamie and Dakota had finished their farewell and were now waiting for Ajay and I to as well. Following him out the house, I stood by Jamie's side and watched as he got into the car. Just as Dakota pulled away from the curb both boys looked towards us and waved. We waved back and wished them a safe trip home before turning and heading back inside.

"Come on, let's put your stuff upstairs," Jamie said lifting up my duffel bag that I had previously dropped in the foyer when we came. I took the bag from her and reprimanded her for even bothering to lift my bag. Even though it wasn't at all heavy as there was only a week's wear of clothing and a small bag of toiletries there was no way I was letting her risk doing such a thing when she was carrying my nephew.

She rolled her eyes in response, "I am pregnant, not cripple," she said falling instep beside me as we made it upstairs to her half of the house—as she liked to call it.

"Well you might as well be if you think I am gonna let you do anything that could possibly harm my little nephew," I grinned at her as we made it up the stairs.

"I swear, you're gonna have him so spoiled," she murmured with a smile on her face.

"Of course, he'll be treated like the little prince he is," I said pushing open her door and following her inside of her room.

I loved her room. It was the second biggest bedroom in the house. The walls were white with crazy splatters of black paint everywhere. I imagined this would be the very result of locking Cruella De Ville in here with a couple buckets of black and white paint.

I flopped down on her bed and looked around at her room. The opposite wall held a bulletin board with a collage of photos, some in black and white and some in color, "Jamie, who did the walls in your room?" I asked propping my head up with my elbows.

"I did," she said, easing into a chair at her desk.

I turned to look at her to see if there was any hint of a smile playing on her face. Realizing there was none I took her seriously, "Your mom let you splat black paint on to your walls?" I asked as I admired her walls again with a new dynamism.

"Yeah, I love art so she said I could spice up my room as long as I didn't do any damage and it wasn't too expensive, I used a half full bucket of paint from the garage and an old paintbrush."

I looked over at the collage of photographs and I had an idea of who took them but I had to ask anyway, "So those are yours?"

She looked over to where I was staring intently and nodded her head in approval, "Yeah, I dabble a bit in photography."

"Well you're really talented," I spoke to her coming off the bed to peer at the pictures at a closer focus, "you're in photography class right?" I asked remembering that she had told me she was indeed taking that class.

"Thanks, yeah, I wanna maybe minor in Photography and major in Fine Art when I go to college," she said shrugging.

"I think you should, you'd be a great artist, your works are really quaint, you know," admiring a picture of a black and white sunset.

Never before had I seen a black and white sunset. Whenever I thought of dusk I thought of pretty colors. I thought of vibrancy, but something about this picture made me want to have been there and see the moment myself. This picture made me feel overwhelmed with a feeling of longing, like I needed to see color. I couldn't quite define the feeling but it made me realize just how beautiful a sunset can be and how hard it was to grasp the fact that there was a sunset drained of its beautiful color.

"I love this one," I said holding it up for her to see, "Why is it in black and white?" I asked.

She smiled knowingly as she answered, "Imagine what it would feel like if all of a sudden you could only see black and white. But you remembered what it's like to see in color. You can easily make out tones and realize that some things are more intense than others, but then nothing is done justice. It becomes frustrating, wouldn't it? I mean how do you feel looking at that picture?"

"Yeah, I do feel sort of deprived, it makes me want to sit and watch a sunset now and savor all the color and beauty . . . and whatnot," I said as I put the picture back onto the board with the rest of the pictures.

Taking that as her cue, she sat up and folded her legs under her in her chair, a big smile crept its way onto her features as she stared expectantly up at me. I knew she was going to want to hear the rest of the story.

As I told her the rest of my adventures for the day, I couldn't help but wonder what Ajay was up to.

Ajay's P.O.V

I feel as though a weight has been lifted. The fact that she forgave me instead of running away like she had been doing since the week began is relieving in itself. I'm stressed out enough as it is, not like I can afford to lose a friend now.

I was sitting up in the top bunk bed in Dakota's room, because sleep was currently unachievable. It was late, past midnight for sure and everyone else was probably asleep. Dakota's light snores made me decide against waking him.

Lord knows I need a friend right now, with all the stuff that was coming at me, a firm foundation to lean on would be welcomed with open arms. I've recently been burdened with a house and payment of bills, though my uncle offers to pay more than half I still have to juggle jobs, thankfully on a weekend. I have been left a hefty sum of money by my parents in a trust fund but unfortunately I can't access it until I am twenty one. So I have to look forward to finishing school and finding an alternative way to pay for college. And if all that wasn't enough, I just found out I am going to be a father. At this point I was almost numb to it all.

Dragging my hand down my face I had to refrain from letting out a frustrated groan. How was I supposed to deal with all of this? At least the drama with Brooklynn is all over though. That was tiring. I have never had to run down a girl to apologize before. I still can't believe she thought that I was using her. Ok well I do believe it, I have a reputation for stuff like that, but that doesn't mean she had to fall victim to the lies. Yes lies, I may be a bit of a ladies' man, but never have I ever cheated on, used or intentionally hurt any of my girlfriends. I do however, move on fast. It's true that I have a new girl almost every week, but in all fairness to me, those girls were all air headed and couldn't hold intelligent conversations, either that or they just weren't the ones for me.

And yes I have broken the law a few times. Nothing serious as everyone makes it out to be, I have never murdered anyone or any of the outrageous things that people have rumored about me. I have outstanding payments for a few speeding tickets and I ditch school every once in a while, but again in all fairness to me, it's not like I am stupid, I could teach the teachers. Not to brag, but I am way smarter than everyone thinks. My uncle doesn't have a PhD in Education for nothing.

But I digress, I'm not sure I understand why Brooklynn thinks I would hurt her. Other than those spurious rumors, I know she has her own personal reason as to why I would intentionally hurt her. Sometimes I don't understand her logic, but whatever. I know she has trust issues, but really c'mon; do I look like I would hurt her? Now it's going to take forever to regain her trust. It's like I am back at square one. I liked it when she trusted me. I got to see a part of her I'm certain not many other people got to see. It made me feel special and privileged. I really enjoy her company; she's so naïve, I can't help but want to corrupt her, yet protect her at the same time . . . if that made any sense. I guess it doesn't, but it was true.

And the fact that she let me into her house to spend the night twice is proof of her naivety. What girl in their right mind let's a guy they barely know with a reputation like mine into their house for a night, let alone two? Okay, so I am glad she did because I really had fun at our sleepovers. One thing I like about her is that she listens to me; I don't get a willing or even caring audience most of the times to listen to me speak my mind so it was refreshing.

I couldn't help but smile as I remembered the two times I had, as she put it, 'sexually harassed' her. At first it was just a joke to see how she'd react since I knew she's never had a boyfriend. I can't remember the line between joke and seriousness because all thoughts of seducing her for fun flew out of my mind then. I couldn't help but notice I loved the way she fit in my arms and it didn't hurt that she's beautiful. No, I am not in love, but I am definitely attracted to her. I'm a guy, it's expected.

Brooklynn's POV

"He came up to me as soon as I left here. Then he begged for forgiveness and all that jazz," I said wanting to get to the part spent at my house, "When we got to my house we talked and hung out," I smiled remembering it.

"What did you talk about?" Jamie asked leaning forward looking more excited than I was.

I smiled at her eagerness and continued.

"Well we were discussing my nephew and him being a father and all, and then he told me about Tristan and Dakota and your relationship, which reminds me there was something I was meaning to ask you," I told her, purposefully leaving out the part about his parents. Maybe she already knew and maybe she didn't, but I don't think Ajay would appreciate me discussing his personal business after he had wholly confided in me.

"Our relationship?" she questioned with a raised eyebrow.

"I had told him you both must have made a perfect couple since you're both so much alike," I said to which she snorted in response, "Ok, I'm guessing you think differently," I suggested, curious as to what she thought about their relationship.

I tried to remember if she had ever talked about their relationship before, but nothing much came to mind.

"We were far from the perfect couple; my relationship with Ajay was more like a friendship more than anything else. We were always laughing and joking around and if not that we were bickering childishly. That was basically it, no spark or anything. Sure there was attraction but that was the only thing keeping us together I guess. Then when we had sex and woke up the next morning feeling disgusted we realized that a relationship wasn't for us," she explained shrugging her shoulders.

I didn't feel so bad hearing Ajay's side now that I had heard hers. Apparently they both felt the same way and no hard feelings were kept. Ajay forgave her for not telling him about her being pregnant with their baby and now they were just friends awaiting the child they conceived.

I told her what Ajay had told me and she nodded her head in agreement then asked, "How does he feel about being a father?"

I smiled in memory of what he had told me, "he said he had no idea of how to even start being a father, but he was going to try to be the best father he could possibly be to his son."

She smiled at this and so did I. Ajay, despite what people thought of him and what his reputation portrayed him to be, was actually one of the sweetest people I have ever met. Two months ago if you had told me that Ajay Edison was going to be a father I would have probably rolled my eyes in indifference and say, "it was bound to happen." Then if you were to tell me he was willing to father the child and be there for it I would have laughed at your stupidity.

Now all I can do is smile in appreciation at Ajay's continuing act of proving me wrong. It was so obvious that he couldn't wait to be a father, the best father to his son. Jamie was fortunate to have her eighteen year old, rebellious ex, father-to-be of her child being so willing to be a part of their baby's life.

The rest of the night was spent watching television; we didn't stay up late because we had to attend school the following morning.

November 23—Thursday

Classes that day were short and void of much learning or teaching. The musical was still an obstacle to overcome with so many students participating; it left most of my classes through the day sparse.

"Can I sit here?" a voice asked above me.

I looked up from doodling on my notebook to see Tristan Jacobs standing over me. It took me a slow moment to realize that he was talking to me and had asked my permission to sit it the empty chair to my left.

"Sure," I replied confused as to why he would want to sit near me.

We were in the middle of fourth period and he had gotten up from his seat in the back to come and sit next to me even when there were many empty chairs about the room. We had never talked before, what made him want to start now? Did he feel obliged to talk to me since Ajay and Dakota did?

Deciding that it would be ill-mannered to ask him why he had chosen to come sit beside me I kept quiet and continued doodling in my notebook. He broke the silence a few moments later though.

"I never got to introduce myself on Sunday. Hi, my name is Tristan Jacobs, and you are?" he asked extending a hand towards me.

I looked down at his extended hand then back at him before I took his hand in my own, "I'm Brooklynn, pleased to meet you," I replied.

"Yes I know, you're the reason Ajay couldn't sleep these past few nights," he said nodding his head.

My eyes widened at his accusation, "Me? What did I have to do with anything?!" I asked incredulously.

"Don't look so appalled, you should be flattered that he can't sleep because of you," he responded.

"How would that make me feel flattered? I feel horrible," I told him.

"You shouldn't, all he's been talking about is how he was going to get you to forgive him, and in all my years of knowing Ajay, not once has he ever wanted a girl's reprieve so badly," he said with a small smile.

"So I've been told," I muttered as I remembered Ajay himself telling me that.

"He doesn't really care for much people and you're one of the few that he does care about," he stated in a serious tone.

I opened my mouth to reply, but I didn't have anything to say so I closed my mouth and opted to listen instead.

"I really don't want to see my best friend get hurt Brooklynn," he said with a sigh.

I nodded in understanding and admiration for the fact that Tristan cared so deeply for his friend.

"Neither do I," I responded.

His smile grew and he nodded in understanding. He knew he wouldn't have to worry about me being the cause of Ajay's pain. It surprised me how they, meaning Ajay, Tristan and Dakota, were dangerous, delinquent guys yet they were such softies and sweethearts under their tough exteriors.

The remaining minutes of the period found us laughing and chatting away in the process of developing a friendship. As soon as the bell rang he had asked me if I wanted to eat lunch with them, but I had to decline since I always ate with Jamie.

"You can ask her if she wants to join us too," he suggested as we gathered up our stuff.

"I'll do that. Where do you eat lunch anyway?" I asked.

"Out back under the huge tree in the farthest corner from the school building," he explained.

I nodded picturing the quiet and serenity the oak tree provided since not much people were ever in the back of the school's compound.

"Ok we'll meet you there," I told him deciding I'd ask Jamie to come with me knowing she would since it wasn't in the cafeteria and Dakota was most likely going to be there.

He nodded as we exited the classroom and came into the hall. This was where we parted to go to our other class before lunch.

"See you later," he said heading in the opposite direction to which I responded with a wave of my hand.

Pushing through the doors of the fire escape I paused looking for Jamie. When I spotted her by the bleachers I smiled and made my way over. I stood over her and when she noticed I had not yet sat she looked up.

"What?" she asked her mouth full of food.

"Tristan invited us to eat lunch with them at the back of the school under the huge tree. You wanna go?" I asked hoping she would say yes.

She paused for a moment then began putting away her stuff. I smiled and stooped to help her put her stuff back into her bag. Taking her bag, I grabbed her arms and helped her up.

"How far along are you?" I asked turning to look at her as we began to walk to the back of the school.

"Almost three months, why?" she asked turning to face me as we walked.

"I was just wondering why you can't tell that you're pregnant," I stated the reason behind my curiosity.

"Most women start swelling around four or five months, but I'm still flat for three, the doctor said that's common too. Some people don't even start until really late in their pregnancy. I'm just happy that I can keep it a secret for a little longer," she informed me

I knew she had to leave school after a certain time, I'm not sure when but I know that it's coming soon, it was dangerous to stay in a school's environment when you're pregnant so they gave her a limit to how long she could stay during her pregnancy.

Nodding to myself and trying to mentally calculate how much more time she had before she left, I almost didn't notice we had turned the corner and as he said, Tristan was sitting under the huge oak tree along with Dakota and Ajay.

"Hey guys," Tristan called as we neared them.

I smiled in response as Jamie waved and went directly over to Dakota where she sat very closely beside him. Tristan was seated not too far from them and patted the ground next to him beckoning me over. I walked over and plopped down next to him seeing nothing wrong with it.

Ajay was standing, leaning against the tree with a distant expression on his face with a lit cigarette hanging lazily from the side of his mouth. He didn't seem to notice that Jamie and I had joined them and if he did he ignored it.

Shrugging, I turned to Tristan and asked him how his science project was coming along. If I remembered correctly he was partnered off with Casey Lamarck and Casey wasn't one of those that cared much for his grades. I was willing to think that Tristan had a case on his hand trying to get Casey to pull his weight with the project.

"It's going better than I first expected it to," he said with a small smirk playing on his lips.

I cocked my head to the side implying my confusion, "What are you talking about?"

"Let's just say that Casey and I have reached an understanding about the project," he told me the smirk widening into a mischievous grin.

"What did you do to him?" I asked appalled at the possibilities.

Looking at my horror stricken face he lifted his hands up and waved them while shaking his head, "No, no. I didn't do anything bad to the kid I just threatened to rearrange his face if he thought that he would leave me to do the whole thing on my own," he told me as if that would quell my worries.

"And how is that not doing anything bad?" I inquired.

"It's better than actually knocking him out isn't it?"

I sighed knowing I couldn't win. I glanced up and my gaze landed on a distant Ajay. His face was turned away from the group and his expression was void of much emotion as he stared blankly ahead of him at nothing in particular. He released a heavy sigh and a tendril of steam curled from his lips, not from the cigarette but from his natural body heat meeting the chilly November air.

Tristan's voice brought me back to paying attention to our conversation, "Where's your lunch?" he asked noticing I didn't have any food with me.

"I had a really big breakfast this morning, so I'm not all that hungry," I said shrugging feeling slightly bad for blatantly lying to him; truth was I hadn't eaten anything that morning.

He looked at me disbelievingly and his smirk turned into a small frown, "Are you anorexic Brooklynn?" he asked abruptly.

That threw me off guard; it was so bluntly stated, well he had asked, but he looked so adamant that it could have been a confident statement. Besides, why did everyone automatically jump to the conclusion that I had an eating disorder when it came to me and my phobia? I'm not even skinny! I'm not fat either, but I wouldn't consider myself skinny. I was just right.

"No," I firmly stated having just enough self control to keep myself from rolling my eyes.

Seeing his look of disbelief I added, "If I feel hungry later on today then I'll eat something."

He paused before he nodded his head deciding to leave the matter as it was.

Lunch came and went along with the rest of the day and I hadn't spoken to Ajay at all. The rest of lunch was just aimless chatter with Tristan with Jamie and Dakota speaking when directly asked a question, but Ajay stayed in his distant reverie and refused to partake in any conversation while we were there that is. I had none of my classes with him so it's not like I could have asked him what the matter was. Jamie didn't seem to notice and I didn't bother to ask her because she was walking around smiling like she was on cloud nine since Dakota had asked her out for tomorrow night.

Next week would be the last week of school before Christmas break began and tomorrow was my last day for sleeping over at the Austins'. I'd miss the homey feel when I left to go back to my own house. I doubted my mother was back from her trip and if she was she didn't call to say that she was so I can say I wasn't missed.

"I can't wait, I wonder where we're going?" she asked herself, pausing to think.

"C'mon Jamie, it isn't exactly warm out here," I told her walking back to grab her hand and pull her along with me.

"Maybe we'll go to a rock concert, I know how much he likes music," she wondered aloud.

It's true that he did love music, mainly rock, but Jamie didn't and I know Dakota wouldn't take Jamie to a place of his preference on their first. He was too much of a gentleman and respected and cared for Jamie too much to neglect her wants and interests. Besides I knew for a fact that he was taking her to an art gallery that was opening tomorrow evening.

"You'll see when he takes you, don't try to spoil the surprise, now come on," I told her tugging on her arm as she had paused mid-step to ponder once again.

It was towards the end of November, and it was very cold, almost freezing. Snow wasn't falling yet, but it would be soon enough.

"Sorry," she apologized as she sped up her pace and I was thankful because her house had come into view as we turned the corner.

Closing the door behind me and following Jamie to the kitchen, my own thoughts wandered as I replayed the conversation at lunch today. Ajay hadn't spoken at all, in fact he didn't even acknowledge my presence and I was beginning to think that maybe he was angry with me for something I wasn't even aware of. But thinking back to our last conversation I can't think of anything that I had done to make him angry or act the way he was acting today.

I wasn't going to ask her anything about it, but right as I was about to reach for a mug to make some hot chocolate Jamie hit me with the question that had been running through my mind all day.

"Don't you think Ajay was acting differently today?" she asked sitting on a bar stool.

I turned around to face her, but I didn't see any sign of craftiness on her face, "what do you mean by different?" I asked her watching to see if her expression had changed at the question.

The same innocent look on her face didn't change as she answered, "He looked kind of distant at lunch, and he didn't really talk to anyone so it was sort of odd. Didn't you notice?" she asked.

"I did, but I thought that maybe he just needed his space or something," I guessed aloud taking down another mug.

This time she rolled her eyes in response, "Space, please, that's the last thing he wants," she stated confidently.

"What makes you say that?" I asked her.

"Well for as long as I have known him, which wasn't that long really, Ajay only acts like that when he wants someone to talk to, something is probably on his mind."

I nodded taking the possibility into consideration. He and I only knew each other for a short time, but most of what I knew about him was from what he told me. There were little things I picked up from his actions as well, but I didn't have so much time spent with him to be able to understand his emotions through the way he acted. For that I would rely on Jamie and judging by the way she paused on 'someone' and looked directly at me I was guessing she wanted me to talk to him.

"You want me to talk to him?"

"Yes, I do. Find a quiet place and have a conversation, find out what's bothering him."

"Why can't you do it?" I asked reaching for the milk in the fridge.

"Cause you two are perfect for each other, who else would be better to do it than you?" she asked as she swiveled around in her bar stool.

I stood agape at her as she spun around in her seat. I couldn't find anything to say in response to that, but she beat me to it and continued on with her blatant words.

"Oh, don't look at me like that; you and I both know that you two are gonna get together," she stated with a huge smile.

"No I don't know that, because we aren't. We can't get together," I told her.

"Why? If you think that I'd object then go ahead because I am giving you full support."

"No it's not that, Ajay and I are just two totally different people who—"

"Are meant for each other," she exclaimed before I could finish my sentence.

Sighing I continued to stir the hot chocolate to sweet perfection. There was no use influencing her otherwise when she had already set her mind to something. Jamie was bent on me and Ajay being together.

"I don't want to get into a relationship anyway," I relied onto her as I brought her a steaming mug.

She was silent for a moment thinking of what to say to my statement, "why not?" she asked.

"I've never been in one before."

"There's a first time for everything," she countered.

"And I don't think I'm ready for one yet either," I went on as if she hadn't interrupted me, "And I don't think he's ready for one either. Jamie, he just found out he's going to be a father," I said trying to find a reason why a relationship between us wouldn't work, but Jamie just wouldn't have that . . .

"I'm going to be a mother and I'm with Dakota. Stop trying to find a way out of this woman. There is so much chemistry going on between you two. Everyone else can see it, but you."

I almost sputtered all over the countertop. Swallowing the hot liquid I took a breath before turning to her. The amused expression she had didn't help anything either.

"What chemistry?" I asked her in bewilderment.

Her eyes performed a 360 degree turn as if I was the one talking nonsense.

What chemistry? Ajay and I have nothing going on between us. We are nothing more than friends.

Yeah, friends with benefits . . .

. . . I thought you died.

"Brooklynn, you two maybe friends now, but there is an obvious connection between you two, you're just blind to it," she said with a sympathetic smile which annoyed me even more.

I sighed in resignation, what's the point in arguing with her when I knew she couldn't be swayed.

November 24—Friday

Fridays were always my favorite day of the week. Last day of school and the anticipation of weekend excitement hung in the air. Even though I knew I had nothing planned, the enthusiasm that buzzed around school was contagious. That same buzz had been going on since the end of October seeing as everyone began to count down the days until school let out for Christmas holidays.

Jamie and I had walked to school again that morning despite the biting atmosphere because her mother had worked a night shift and we didn't want to bother her for a ride to school. Maybe it was an unspoken understanding because as soon as we entered the halls of our high school Tristan and Dakota fell casually in step with us. I could understand Dakota's presence he and Jamie were an item now, but Tristan . . . ? And where was Ajay?

"Morning" Tristan stated from my left.

"Hey," I replied, "Is Ajay here?"

"Yeah, he's out back," Tristan stated casually.

I wondered if I should venture outside to seek him out, or maybe he really wanted to be alone. I know that Jamie said that he didn't, but wouldn't his friends know he was seeking comfort and talk to him? I didn't want to go to him and have him turn his back on me.

I looked around and realized I would feel much more comfortable if Ajay were with us. Why? Because he was my friend and friends are supposed to be there for each other. Sighing lightly I turned to Tristan since Jamie was too wrapped up in her lover's words to notice anything else.

"I think I'm gonna go find Ajay," I told Tristan as I turned around.

I left them and began heading to the school's rear exit, but not before I saw the satisfied smile on Tristan's face.

Pushing open the doors, the chilly wind engulfed me and my skin reacted with goose bumps. Hopefully I could get Ajay to come inside where the temperature was much warmer. I spotted him over by the tree we hung out at yesterday and strode over to him. He was pretty much holding the identical position as he was yesterday at lunch. Leaning against the tree, one hand in his pocket and the other waiting patiently at his side to occasionally pull out the cigarette he was inhaling. His face was expressionless, but his eyes held a mixture of confusion and frustration.

I stood there for about two whole minutes not exactly knowing how to start the conversation I was playing out in my head. It was slightly unsettling too, the fact that Ajay knew I was there yet he wasn't making an attempt to acknowledge my presence. I didn't allow myself to feel hurt, but I was questioning myself. Maybe he really wanted to be alone and I was just intruding. But I couldn't bring myself to go either. So deciding it was now or never I blurted out.

"We're friends right?" I don't know what brought me to ask that. I just blurted it out on impulse.

His head turned to me and the look in his eyes told me he wasn't expecting that.

Well neither was I

Of course you're friends!

Seriously, I thought you died . . .

"Do you remember the last conversation we had?" he asked pulling the nicotine wrap away from his lips.

I paused for a moment, and then nodded as I remember the day before yesterday when we were talking in Jamie's foyer before he left to go home with Dakota.

"I've been thinking about it," he said.

I paused again wondering what about that conversation between us would have him acting so distant and reclusive from everyone. Hopefully it wasn't anything I had said to instill this in him.

"What exactly were you thinking about?" I asked looking at the way his stance appeared to be burdened.

"I didn't know I came off as such a terrible guy to you-"

"You're not a bad person Ajay, I told you that," I interrupted him wanting to get that straight.

"Well, you said I wasn't trustworthy," he went on.

I couldn't respond to that, because I had told him that. I didn't trust him as much as I used to.

"And it got me to thinking about some stuff and I really want to change your mind," he continued.

"If this is about that friends trusting friends thing, then don't worry about it. You're a great friend, I just have major trust issues," I stated.

His lips turned up at the corners in a small smirk, "That's not what I was thinking about, but thanks, you're a great friend too."

I smiled at that. *Yay*! He told me I was a great friend.

"Then what is it that you're thinking about that has to do with me trusting you?" I queried in curiosity.

He put the cigarette to his lips again, inhaled deeply then let it go before he answered, "Remember how I told you that my parents got killed?"

I nodded, how could I have forgotten something like that? It was only two days ago since I heard, I knew it was a rhetorical question, but still . . .

"I didn't give you the entire story," he paused and I inclined my head fully ready to hear what he was about to tell me, "They owned the company and it basically ran itself, they never really went into the office unless there were important board meetings and they were required to be there and even then they usually did it via web cams. They travelled too, but not too much; they wanted to be good parents to their only son so they tried to be home as much as possible while running their business."

I had no idea where this was going or what it had to with trust, but I listened giving him my undivided attention.

"They were home a lot and I was beginning to feel crowded and rebellious, I just wanted them out of the house for a while. I was so stupid, I wanted them gone then maybe I could have gone to the arcade with Tristan and Dakota or something," I wanted to tell him that he wasn't stupid, that he was just young, but I knew he wanted me to listen so I stayed quiet, "I told them they missed a call from one of the board directors requesting them at work for a hugely important decision making conference.

"It was planned out too. It was so easy to manipulate technology back then so I changed the numbers in their contact list and listed my own number under the director's name. So when they checked their phones there was a message from "the director" requesting them immediately. Looking back on it I can't believe I did all that just to get them out of the house for a little while. They left to go to the office and I got ready to go to the arcade, but it started raining so we couldn't go anymore. We were only thirteen at the time so we had to walk and Dakota's and Tristan's folks wouldn't let them walk in the rain and they couldn't drive us, besides that meant that I'd have to get permission from my folks to go and that didn't make any sense after all I'd done to get them out of the house. I knew I'd get in trouble when they realized I lied to them. So I stayed at home and waited for them to come back, but they never did."

I felt a burning sensation in my heart. Before he finished I could tell where he was going and I couldn't bring myself to believe the type of agony he must have been experiencing.

"My uncle called later that night and told me that a troubled employee had come in and went on a fatal rampage that day. He'd bought a house and a car on the belief that he would have gotten a promotion. When he didn't get it, he realized he had put himself in nearly irreversible debt. Angry and desperate he came into the office the following day armed and with a vengeance," he stopped, his eyes holding an insurmountable amount of torture.

I wanted to hug him to hold him and wish away all his sadness. But I made no move to do anything since I could tell he wasn't yet finished.

"Right before they left my dad turned to me and asked if I was sure I'd be okay with them leaving and I told them that they couldn't look over me forever. I practically lead them to their graves. I was so stupid, I lied to get them out of the house for one day, but now they're gone forever. I was so stupid. I betrayed their trust and got them killed. I will never be able to forgive myself for lying to them and betraying their trust . . . I-it's my fault they died," he choked as he finished.

I just couldn't hold back this time. I immediately stepped forward and embraced him in a firm hug making sure I got across the point that I was there for him fully. To be put through such mental and emotional torture at such a tender age was just unfathomable to me. How could he think that it was his fault they were murdered? It wasn't his fault at all; fate just has a crazy way of working things.

I felt his arms wrap around me, returning the embrace, and I wanted to cry for him and with him. I held back the tears as I squeezed a little tighter. It wasn't fair for him to be going through this trauma. Then again life was never fair. Yet, I couldn't help but be angry at God for letting this happen to him and all people who have ever suffered.

"Brooklynn, I am truly sorry for losing your trust, I never meant to hurt you. That was never my intention. But please believe me when I say I will try my hardest to get you to trust me and if I ever lie to you it will only be for your own good. I promise I will never intentionally do anything to hurt you in anyway," he told me with the most sincere voice. I couldn't see his face since we were still in our embrace and it was buried in my hair.

When we did pull away however his face was tear free, I knew he was trying to be strong and not cry and I admired the strength he had, I'd be bawling my liver string out after telling that story. Then I realized why he told me and what the reason was.

"Ajay, it doesn't matter that you think it is; it's not your fault and I know you didn't try to hurt me and if you're worrying that you'll hurt me in the future, then stop 'cause I know you won't," I firmly stated staring straight into his eyes.

I could tell he didn't believe a word I was saying; he was firm in his belief that he'd somehow be the cause of my downfall like he thought he was the cause for his parents'. But I would get him to put those thoughts out of his mind. Those thoughts were dangerous ones to have. I didn't exactly want him walking around treating me like fragile china either. I knew that would get irritating over a very short period of time. But putting that aside. How many burdens could a person possibly carry? I thought just going to school was a job all on its own and I needed a break from that, but now I'm appreciating the fact that it's only school I have to predominantly worry about. In his unfortunate case, school had to be the least of his worries, with a house to upkeep, bills to pay, two jobs, a baby along the way and the mental agony of believing his parents death was somehow his fault. I don't know how he bears it all and keeps sane or at least look so calm and collected on the outside.

His maturity level awes me. Only at the age of eighteen with so many things forcing him to grow up and act older than he really was. Overwhelming doesn't even begin to describe how that only sounds. Glancing up into his eyes again I could tell that he was tired. Emotionally tired and how could anyone blame him? I was exhausted from just imagining what he has to go through.

Just as I was about to suggest that we head back into the warmth of the building the bell rang sounding the beginning of the academic day. No worries though, since last week where rehearsals have been going on infinitely it seemed classes just stopped. It was a gradual thing too. Teachers came to school, they just didn't bother to teach anything. It was the second to last week of school anyway what was the point in teaching when half the class wasn't there and also when most of the children would forget over the winter vacation just to have to come back and learn it all over again when the new semester started?

Walking side by side we left the chilly November air behind as well as my previous perception I had of Ajay. As time went by I learned that I gained more respect for him. I realized he wowed me in ways I just never expected and made me think differently about a lot of things.

We hadn't even turned the corner of the first hallway when we met up again with Tristan, Dakota and Jamie. Well, actually we met up with Tristan, the two lovebirds were trailing a few feet behind totally oblivious to the world outside their own.

"What class do you have now?" Ajay asked me, he didn't turn to me or anything, but I'm positive he knows which class Tristan had so I am assuming he could only be talking to me.

"You got him to talk!" Tristan gasped, wide eyed, but I couldn't tell if he was serious or joking so I wasn't sure how to reply.

In response to Ajay's question though I told him I had I.T. He nodded but didn't make any move to suggest I stay or go. I was about to head off, when Tristan turned to me and asked, "So where are we headed?"

I opened my mouth to respond, but yet again I was not sure how to respond to that. I was going to class, I didn't know about them.

"Wait, where are *you* going?" Tristan queried.

That I could answer, "To class."

The look upon his face made me ask, "Aren't you?"

Instead of answering he turned to a still quite silent Ajay and remarked, "Aw, she's so naïve. She's cute, you should keep her."

I'm not sure if I should have been insulted or what by that statement. Naïve? How was that being naïve? If they weren't heading to class, then where were they going? It wouldn't make much sense to ditch out under the bleachers when your fingers begin to turn numb after only five minutes of air exposure. I couldn't think of anywhere else to go when ditching a class other than the music room which was in use by the rehearsing students of the Christmas play, they were rehearsing to perform next week.

I stayed silent and Ajay and Tristan led the way through a few hallways, up two stairwells and down another three hallways. I never noticed before, but our school was pretty massive. I had never even been to this part of the school. None of my classes required venturing up here either so it's plausible. Then again I don't think much or any classes were even held up in this section of the school, but by the way Tristan and Ajay navigated their way through the hallway like they'd been here before confirmed my belief that this must have been a usual thing. As much as I respect and see him in a new perspective, there is no denying his rebellious ways. This was the main reason why so many girls swooned at just the sound of his name. Something about that edgy, don't care attitude did a number on many girls. I can't say it didn't affect me too, because it did.

Just a few seconds and footsteps later we were standing outside of a metal door, similar to the many doors located all over the school. Upon opening the door, I saw that it led to a classroom; at least I think it was a classroom. There were no desks or tables anymore, but the evidence of a dry erase board was all that I needed to make the right guess. The room was slightly dusty, with the occasional cardboard box strewn around. There were also two crates that were near to each other in back of the room against the wall. I am guessing it was used as makeshift chairs and I was proved right when they both went forward and prepared to sit on them.

I walked over to the window, looking out to see exactly where in the building I was located. I could see into the back of the next door house's backyard which had a pool that I am pretty sure would be excruciatingly freezing. I didn't even know the school had a next door neighbor; it's just the way the school was built I couldn't really see who located the lot adjacent to it.

Turning away from the window I approached the two and noticed that there was nowhere for me to sit. I didn't really expect them to get up and offer me a seat which they didn't, yet I did maybe think that one of them would scoot over and offer me part of their seat which, still, none of them did. I was about to demand one of them to move over when Ajay looked up at me expectantly.

"What?" he asked.

"Can you move over please?" I queried politely.

"Why?" he asked.

I had to admit I was taken aback by the boldness of the inquiry. I didn't think he'd be cruel enough to make me stand.

"So I can sit," I offered.

His eyebrows furrowed a bit then his head cocked slightly to the side, "You can sit here," he said.

"Where?" I wanted to know, as he wasn't pointing to anything.

Instead of answering he patted his lap and it took me a while to realize he wanted me to sit in his lap. I almost laughed thinking he was joking, but looking at the expression I thought better of it and answered, "no, seriously, move over."

"Either you sit here, or you stand," he replied.

"Or you can sit here," Tristan piped in referring to his own lap.

Rolling my eyes I surrendered and placed myself lightly on Ajay not wanting to burden him with my full weight. Out of seemingly nowhere, his hands wrapped around my waist and pulled me further into him, "Really, you're light as a feather, stop being shy and get comfortable," he said.

I did after a few moments of hesitation, but after those few moments, conversation flowed and I began to relax while I conversed and shared jokes with the both of them. Once or twice I fleetingly wondered about Jamie and Dakota, but I knew they were having a great time without us.

I was really proud of Jamie to be able to make the best of her situation like she was doing. A lot of girls our age faced with the problem of pregnancy wouldn't be able to handle it as well as she was. I admired her more than she knew for that, for I knew that I included wouldn't be able to hold on to the hope she had for so long.

I jumped slightly when I felt Ajay's fingers nip my side. Turning to face him with a look of surprise and irritation he answered, "Where were you, Tristan just asked you something," he explained.

"Sorry, what was that?" I apologized turning to Tristan listening for his question this time.

"I was asking if you wanted to come over to my house this weekend. Casey and I have to work on our assignment and I thought that maybe you guys might wanna do yours too," he suggested looking at both Ajay and I for our responses.

If I said yes then this would be the second time that I would have been in is house; last time wasn't so delightful, but I am pretty sure that this time wouldn't be affected by the last.

Nodding my head at Tristan for him to know that I had accepted his invite I began to doubt if it were really work related reasons he invited us over for. Knowing these guys, I was aware that they weren't exactly eager about academics. Hopefully it wasn't another party he was hosting, effects of last time or not, I wouldn't have enjoyed that party. It's just not my thing.

Probably having seen the look on my face he said, "Don't worry, we really are going to be working on our projects. I just wanna get it out of the way so I don't have to deal with Casey anymore," Tristan reassured me.

"What's wrong with Casey?" I asked knowing that he was a bit delinquent, but I also knew Tristan scared him out of that so I don't see what more could be wrong with him.

"He annoys the shit outta me!" Tristan stated exasperatedly.

"Yeah, but how?" I asked.

"He's just so . . . he's always talking about Kimora. If it's not about how pretty she is, it's about how he wants to date her," he said, sounding frustrated.

"I don't see what's so wrong with that," I stated slightly shaking my head.

"What's wrong is that she's my girlfriend," he explained briefly.

"Since when?" I blurted out, now finding out that the pretty Japanese girl and Tristan were together.

The amused smile on Tristan's face left me blushing at my ignorance of the apparently obvious.

"Well how am I supposed to know who people in this school date?" I tried to defend myself knowing it was a futile attempt.

"News travels faster than the speed of light around here. The question is how could you not know?" Tristan countered with a smirk.

"Well excuse me for not sticking my nose in your business, I had no idea it was recommended," I answered sarcastically.

Seriously, who in their right minds wants their business spread all over the school?

"You hang out with Ajay; I thought he'd at least tell you."

This time the subject of our conversation spoke up from behind me, "Because we have nothing better to talk about, but you and your current girl."

"Of course not, you spend all your time together talking about how devilishly handsome I am and how you so wish you could look half as stunning as me," he finished by flashing us a toothy grin.

Looking back at Ajay I caught him rolling his eyes at his best friend's antics and I couldn't help but laugh at the two. In the middle of my bout of sudden laughter the shrill sound of the bell rang as a reminder that second period was about to start. Glancing at the both of them I could tell that they weren't even considering the thought of going to their next class. I made to get up anyway, but the grip Ajay had around my middle tightened, pulling me pack down into his lap.

"Where are you going, you have Music next and your teach is at the rehearsal," Ajay spoke into my ear.

How does he know what class I have next?

Grinning at my confused expression and squinted eyes Tristan answered, "He reviewed your schedule, don't worry he's not stalking you . . . yet."

I let out a short breath between a sigh and a laugh getting used to their antics by now, "I'd like to see the day Ajay decides he wants to stalk someone."

I was about to laugh, but stopped myself when I glimpsed Tristan's face. He looked as though he had just remembered something worth sharing with the world which instantly flagged my curiosity.

"What?" I asked.

"No, that incident is not to be repeated to anyone!" Ajay spoke up from behind me.

"What, what happened? Tell me!" I pleaded wanting to be let in on the secret as well because I hated being left out.

Tristan went to open his mouth but it closed right after with a smile tempting me in the most maddening way.

Tell me dammit. I wanna know too!

"Why won't either of you tell me? I thought we were friends now?" I asked with a pout, wanting badly to know about this little secret of theirs.

"We are," they simultaneously replied.

"Then why won't you let me in on the secret?" I asked trying to make them feel guilty.

"I want to tell you, trust me I do, but Ajay's way too embarrassed to let anyone else know about it," Tristan explained smirking at Ajay's expense.

I turned to face Ajay, "You can tell me, I won't laugh. I promise," I told him.

He was glaring at Tristan over my shoulder angry with him for even bringing up the topic, but answered me nonetheless, "You'll laugh," he said.

"I promise I won't," wanting to know if it really was as amusing as they were making it out to be.

I felt him sigh as he considered telling me and I had to keep back a smile of victory knowing he was going to tell me, "When we were in eighth grade," he was referring to Tristan and him, "there was this girl that I had a crush on . . ."

"What was her name?" I interrupted him.

He paused for a moment, hesitant to tell me, "Akaela . . ."

I couldn't help, but to cut him off mid sentence again, "Ramsey!" I blurted out.

He nodded his head and I could hear Tristan try to stifle his laugh behind us.

"You stalked Akaela Ramsey in the eighth grade?" I confirmed and it sounded as bizarre out loud as it did in my mind.

Akaela was the Queen Bee of the high school hierarchy. Always has been and I am pretty sure she always will be. She's not as bad as one thinks she would be with her title and reputation and all. She isn't a superficial bitch, that's for one. Her status doesn't go to her head like most of her little wannabe followers, but she wouldn't look twice at the people who aren't part of her crowd. So it's an odd picture seeing someone like Ajay, unsolved and mysterious Ajay, dressed the way he was now with a Bullet For My Valentine hoodie and black skinny jeans following Akaela, in her Juicy Couture and D&G sunglasses, like a lovesick puppy.

He nodded in resignation sitting back since he had no need to finish telling the story seeing as I had already figured it out. I never would have guessed . . . Akaela Ramsey and Ajay Edison. They were from two totally different worlds; it's completely odd to watch them stand next to each other. The difference is obvious to anyone whose vision isn't impaired.

Glancing behind me I caught the look on his face, "What? I didn't laugh!" I defended myself.

"I know, but I know what you're thinking and that's just as worse," he muttered.

"What am I thinking then?" I questioned.

He paused at my inquiry then spoke, "You think it's weird that I liked her. Probably think we'd never make a good couple," he stated.

"No it's weird that you *stalked* her," I said putting emphasis on the stalk part, "and who am I to decide what kind of couple you'll make, though I'll admit, the thought of you two being together is hard to grasp," I shared with them.

He had nothing to say to that and neither did Tristan which was surprising in itself since, so far, the boy always had something to say. So I decided to throw in my next statement, "It's like trying to imagine me going out with Blake Diego."

"Blake's a promiscuous whore, why would you ever go out with the likes of him?" Tristan spoke up from his perch.

"He is not!" I defended him automatically.

Tristan's eyebrows raised and a small smile of comprehension came to his face, I knew his next words before they came out of his mouth.

"You like him, don't you!" he stated more than asked.

I narrowed my eyes at him in mock anger and stuck out my tongue at him before answering, "I used to, there's a difference."

"What did you see in him?" Ajay asked calmly from behind me, which led me to think that he was asking out of curiosity and not animosity.

"He is like sooo hot! His hair is amazing and his eyes are to die for!"

A horrible imitation of a girl's voice erupted from Tristan as he answered for me.

Rolling my own eyes and giving him a look I said, "No one talks like that, first of all, well at least I don't. But you're right. He does have great hair, it's so curly and his eyes are such a pretty hazel color," I admitted.

"That's all you see in guys?" Ajay asked and his tone sounded slightly accusing.

"No, I was just agreeing with him," I jerked my thumb to the smug looking Tristan, "I liked him because he . . ." I paused, realization dawning, that Ajay was right, that is all I had seen in Blake—his looks.

"Hm, you were saying?" Ajay mocked with a slight smirk on his face.

"Ok, so maybe I only liked him for his looks, but he is a promiscuous man whore after all, so you can't blame me," I smiled.

The smirks on both of their faces led me to ask, "So you mean to tell me, neither of you have ever fallen for just a girl's looks?"

"Nope," Ajay said popping the 'p'.

I looked up at the other boy and waited for his reply, "Well, it was never with a girl's looks," he said.

My head cocked to the side I asked, "What do you mean?"

"I've fallen for a guy because of his outward appearance before," he explained sheepishly.

"You're bisexual?" I asked.

"Somewhat," he shrugged.

My shock was repressed by the memory of Ajay informing me of them having made out before. I was still a little shocked, but now I was mainly confused, I had to ask now before anything else could interrupt me.

"Are you bi too?" I asked directing the question at the boy I was sitting on.

"No," he replied, "I told you, it was just to entertain the girls," he said.

"Oh," I nodded, "Is Dakota-"

"I'm the only one, they're both bone straight," Tristan explained to me.

Once again I nodded, now with my confusion all cleared up I waited patiently for him to continue.

"So anyway, the guy was a work of art, you really should have seen him; grey eyes and blonde hair. Normally I don't go for blondes, but this boy was an Adonis in the flesh," he said with a reminiscent smile, "And every time he smiled you could see his dimple in his left cheek, man I'd still bone him if given the chance," he said with a roguish smirk.

"What's wrong with him then?" I asked repressing the urge to roll my eyes at him.

"Absolutely nothing, he's perfect in every way, great personality, even greater looks . . ."

"I thought you fell for his looks," I stated.

"I did, before I got to know him, and then I fell for him as a person," he told me.

"Does Kimora know about this?" I wanted to know.

"Yeah and she understands, it's like her wanting to jump Jared Leto, for some odd reason," he informed me, making me understand that it was just a crush alone he had for this boy.

"You don't think differently of me now, do you?" he asked after a while of comfortable silence among us three.

"Why would I think—oh because of you being bisexual?" I asked.

He nodded in affirmation.

"Of course not, that doesn't change you or make you any less of the great guy you are," I assured him, "Besides if it makes you feel better, I'll let you in on a little secret."

I knew I had captured their full attention now; the reaction was very similar to how girls act right before they're let in on some good gossip.

"If given the chance, I would totally make out with Megan Fox," I told them knowing their reactions would be priceless.

"What!?" they both chorused at the same time.

Bullet for my Valentine Hoodie . . . $32.

Ditching Music Class . . . possible detention.

But seeing the look on their faces after I told them that . . . was priceless and so worth any detention we could have gotten.

"You told me you hated girl on girl action!" Ajay accused.

"No, I said I don't see what's so great about watching it, I never said anything about doing it," I added just to see their look of shock increase.

"Are you serious?" Tristan asked incredulously.

Of course I was. Have you not seen Megan Fox? The woman is sex on a platter.

I nodded my head in avowal, letting them both know that I was indeed serious. I still don't know why I was sharing this tidbit of information with them, but I felt completely comfortable doing so and I was loving the feeling of freedom to express myself and not having to worry about them judging me on what I did or said.

"What's wrong with me being attracted to her?" I wondered audibly.

143

"Nothing, absolutely nothing," Ajay piped up, "but I never thought you to be, well to be attracted to a girl," he honestly explained.

"Well, most people don't either, and I want to continue letting them think so, this piece of information stays amongst the three of us, understand?" I said firmly.

They both nodded in understanding and agreement. Satisfied, I leaned back into Ajay's chest.

"I'm still surprised," he informed me to which I smiled lightly.

"I know, I just thought that you should know, and also realize that I won't judge you because you're bi, Tristan," I said directing the last part solely to him so he could rest assured that I would never judge him just because of his sexual preferences.

We left our hideout when the bell for lunch rang deciding it would be wise to get something to eat and also try to find Jamie and Dakota. We saw them coming up the stairs possibly coming to seek us out. We all headed towards the cafeteria. Jamie and I always brought lunch, but the boys wanted some stuff there. Walking with them, Jamie fell into step beside me with a faint smile.

"Looks like someone is enjoying her day so far," I teased.

"I am, Dakota is simply the best, he's so sweet and funny and refreshingly candid," she confided in me.

"Well you two should make a great match since you're so frank yourself," I said with a smile watching the way her eyes lit up at the comment.

"I sure hope so."

"Don't worry, everything will work out fine," I reassured her, "Do you know where he's taking you tonight?"

"No, he refuses to tell me and it's so frustrating when he won't even hint anything about it, damn," she said with a playful smile.

"You'll see when we get there," Dakota said from beside Tristan, having overheard her.

Jamie stuck out her tongue at him to which he playfully returned the gesture. Looking at them was like watching a Disney romance. It was cute though. Hopefully it would continue to stay this PG-13. I have no desire to see them groping each other and swapping spit at every interval. That could get annoying fast.

"Why do we even bother to come to school if nothing is going on?" Tristan spoke up from my left.

"Like we have anything better to do at home," Ajay replied.

After a short pause on his part, Tristan answered, "True, but at least let's make coming to school worthwhile."

"How do we make that happen?" Dakota asked.

"I don't know yet, but I'll think of something and hopefully we won't be forced to spend the rest of the day sitting around talking about nothing to kill time," he reassured us.

"Well you do that man, while I go get me some onion rings, does anyone want any?" Ajay asked as we walked through the doors of the cafeteria.

"I'll keep thinking about a plan to keep us occupied as soon as I'm finished with that beautiful lady over there," Tristan informed as he left Dakota, Jamie and I to go over to the table where his girlfriend, Kimora, was sitting at.

"Can you get me a Sprite?" I asked Ajay as he headed over to the cafeteria line.

"Sure," he said.

Now I was left with Dakota and Jamie, who were now looking for a table to sit at. I followed them to a table at the left end of the cafeteria. This was unfamiliar grounds for me since Jamie and I had made it a habit to sit out on the field beneath the bleachers and eat lunch. I can't remember the last time I actually step foot inside the cafeteria with the intent to eat.

We sat and Jamie and Dakota were friendly enough to welcome me into their conversation, but I knew that by the way their eyes were seeking each other that they'd rather talk alone. So I let them. Besides, it wasn't long before Ajay came back with a tray of onion rings, fries and a Sprite.

"I thought you only went for onion rings?" I asked as he slid the Sprite over to me.

"Thanks . . ."

I twisted the cover off and placed the bottle to my lips, Sprite was so refreshing, just a burst of excitement in every sip.

"I did," he replied sliding the potato wedges off of the tray as well and slid them over to me.

I looked at them then at him, "Who are those for?" I asked.

"You," he said with a cute smile as he dipped an onion ring into the white sauce beside it.

I then proceeded to slide the box of fries back to him, "I didn't ask for any."

"You didn't have to," he said pushing it back in front of me.

"But . . ."

"No buts. Eat it," he ordered as he plopped the sauce covered ring into his mouth.

I sighed in resignation as I continued sipping my Sprite. He looked over at me and noticed my action of ignoring the food, "That had better be gone by the time lunch is finished," he playfully threatened.

Rolling my eyes at him I made a show of picking up a fry eating it, "Happy?"

"Don't sass me," he replied faking anger.

"I'll do what I want," I retorted in the same manner.

"You'll eat those fries, is what you'll do," he said pointedly looking at the fries.

I let out a small laugh as I took another fry this time dipping it in ketchup and eating it.

"Good girl," he said patting my head before turning back to his own food.

I decided that I was a little hungry so I did end up eating it all. I ended up sharing my Sprite with Ajay because Dakota ended up stealing his Coke when he wasn't looking.

The academic day ended like it always did; nothing special but welcomed with open arms especially since it was Friday and the weekend officially started when the last bell rang.

As we all left the parking lot, Jamie, Ajay and I on foot and Tristan and Dakota in their respective cars, we all dispersed and headed home. The only thing I had on my agenda for the rest of the evening was sleep and more sleep.

As I entered my room I couldn't help but glance over at the reliable machine sitting atop my desk. It had been a while since I seized the opportunity to relax and use it for anything other than school assignments. Deciding that sleep could take a back burner for a while, I slipped my faithful laptop into its carrying case before heading back out of my room with it slung over my shoulder with the renewed intent of retiring to the empty field that I had dubbed my own.

As I sat there under the lone massive oak tree with the wind blowing my hair every which way, my mind at peace, my thoughts drifted to a certain redhead.

Jamie's P.O.V

I'm almost three months pregnant. The ninth of next month will make it exactly three months. My unborn baby was conceived on the ninth of September of this year. The ninth of the ninth of the ninth what a coincidence, right? I thought my life was officially over.

I'm in my last year of high school and pregnant. How was I going to tell my mother about this? Will I be able to graduate or do I have to drop out? What's going to become of my social life? I don't know the first thing about taking care of a baby.—

Those were just a few of the jumbled thoughts racing through my mind at the time.

You can imagine how worried and scared I was about this whole thing. I was carrying my ex boyfriend's child and he had no idea of it, and I had no intentions of telling him either. The sex we had was meaningless, to the both of us. What was I supposed to do? Stroll up to his locker and say, "Remember when we hooked up a month ago? Well now I'm pregnant and it's yours. You're gonna be a daddy!" I can just imagine how that scene would go down.

What I didn't imagine or expect though was how my 'friends' had taken the news. I thought they'd have my back and comfort me in my time of distress, instead they all looked at me like I was, all of a sudden, an alien because I had another life growing inside of me. Well, when I put it like that I guess it does sound weird, but still. I can't believe I wasted so much years of my life investing trust into our friendship. They simply told me their 'rep' was way too important to get tainted by me getting 'knocked up with a delinquent's kid' . . . their words, not mine.

They were more concerned about their blasted reputation than the likes of their best friend since grade school?! Let me tell you; that hurt me more than I could say. They had all abandoned me and to add insult to an already critical injury, one of them said, "If it makes you feel any better, we won't tell a soul," while the rest of them nodded with synchronized pity.

'If it makes me feel better'? I wanted to kick her. I wanted to kick all of them. *That* might have made me feel better, dammit. But I didn't; I just stood there while they filed out of my bedroom and left. The next day at school was simply awful. They kept true to their word because when I entered the cafeteria and passed by their table, the one I was always welcomed at before, they all ignored me as if I was something that the flipping dog dragged in! Their betrayal stung just as hard as it had the day before. It hurt so badly that I cried . . .

Not in front of them of course, I cried in the girl's bathroom; long and hard until an angel found me. A sweet caring angel by the name of Brooklynn Vladimir; that was on October the ninth. She was a shy lonely sweetheart and she was willing to be my friend, and that is something I will always appreciate.

The tenth of October, I was invited over to her house. It's huge, lemme tell you that now. Her family is loaded, but she doesn't let that get to her head; that I soon learned as I spent more time with her. And the more time I spent with this girl the more I opened up about myself, it was a long and tough process for me, but she made it so much easier. Every time I let something about my life slip to her, she nodded her head and urged me to continue talking. Not once has she ever looked at me with disdain or contempt, she always seems to understand or wants to if she doesn't. What more could I ask for in a friend?

I was still pregnant though, and besides the fact that I did eventually get around to telling my mom about it (strangely enough she was happy about the news), it was still there. The 'it' being this new life form that was slowly, but it was surely growing in my tummy; the 'it' that everyone had dubbed as a 'he'. I've yet to go to the doctor and have the gender of the fetus determined. Apparently, I had to wait until I was further into the pregnancy. I could have also done something called an amniocentesis, but the nurse had mentioned to my mother about the risks of injuring the baby's limbs and she instantly closed her mind to that idea. So the gender of the baby remains unknown, yet for some odd reason everyone wants me to have a boy.

And I keep asking myself, does it matter what *I* want? I know that my wants and needs have been addressed with great attention ever since I learned about this conception. When my mother learned that she would be a grandmother, she went crazy happy and couldn't stop fussing over me about mine and my baby's health, then when Brooklynn learned . . . well she's been a sweetheart from the start so there wasn't any change there, even when Ajay found out his response was filled with enthusiasm (which wasn't at all what I had expected). When I learned I was pregnant, well I won't lie; I was less than ecstatic. The last thought on my mind was *'I'm gonna be a mommy, yay!'*

I was scared out of my mind. I still am. I have all the support that I could need, but I couldn't help but worry about the future and what it'll bring. Am I going have to forgo chasing my dreams to take care of this little person who I don't even know . . . yet? I'd have to take care of the child, send it to school, which means I'd have to get a job. I guess I'd have to save college/university for later. But how much later? How long would I have to keep putting off my life for this baby's?

It's going to be all about the baby, and I know I'm being selfish here, but what about me? Doesn't it matter what I want? What about my life and my future?

Sigh

But I guess I brought this all on myself, right? It's the consequences of unprotected sex. It's not like I didn't know about the penalties either. All those damn prevention commercials and free condoms being tossed at youths all the time, one would have to be living under a rock to not know about the whole situation and how it works. So I couldn't blame my momentary lack of judgment on not being aware, because I was. I was also lazy and too stupid and too intoxicated to even think about all of that when I mindlessly slipped down my panties.

But why is this all my fault? If I remember correctly, Ajay didn't exactly stop and say, "Let's use a condom," either. As far as I know, it takes two people to make a child, so why the hell am I the only one who has to pay? I don't see him having to worry about dropping out of school to give birth, nor does he have to wake up in the morning to the upsetting urge to chuck his stomach's contents out.

My life sucks!

And now I am crying! I wiped at my eyes in frustration. I really am amazed at how I do it; stay so collected and calm on the outside when my emotions are simply out of control. Thank God I was in the confines of my own home though. School was long and tedious today and I really don't care to describe what happened other than, the time I spent with Dakota was amazing and then after lunch it was Tristan's smart idea to play hide and seek. You can just imagine how that went.

I pulled myself off of the sofa that I was currently occupying. If I didn't get started now, I wouldn't have enough time to get ready for the date that Dakota had prepared for us tonight. I still have no idea where it is he's taking me, which means I'm blindly dressing myself tonight.

The doorbell rang and I laughed silently at the great timing the ringer had. Had they waited till I was already upstairs to ring then they would have to just wait or either come back again at a time when I was conveniently already downstairs. You won't believe how winded I get sometimes just to climb the staircase. It's such a task!

Veering off the right into the foyer I reached forward and opened the door only to see my best friend. A smile found its way onto my frustrated face; it's hard not to feel happy whenever I'm around Brooklynn. But I couldn't help but wonder why she was here.

"Come in, you must be freezing," I said realizing that she must be cold having to stand there with just a thin wool jacket on to keep her warm over her clothing.

She briskly walked past me as I shut the door behind her, banning all the cold air to stay out and the air that already slipped inside was soon warmed by the thermostat. She sniffled a bit before she thrust a bag that she was carrying out in front of me.

"Um . . .?" I looked to the bag then to her, I was still confused as to why she was here.

She never mentioned coming over while we were at school. I hope nothing was wrong.

"Take it," she ordered, or well, tried to through the chattering of her teeth.

I looked at her with a skeptical expression before I grasped the handle of the bag and eased it out of her cold fingers. Did she walk all the way here? I know it's a short walk, but it's freezing out.

"What's this?" I asked her glancing into the bag and seeing, what I assumed to be lots of clothes.

"Selections for your date tonight, you didn't think I'd leave you to dress yourself not even knowing where you're going, right?" she asked me with a small smile on her face.

That certain smile always gets to me, she has more than one, but this one in particular I always notice. It's a smile of a person wanting to be accepted. I could see her insecurities, she used that smile often. I doubt she even realizes it though. When she smiles like that I know what it means even if she doesn't, I automatically smile back and she feels at ease again. I detect it in her stance and the obvious way that her smile turns into a normal one, where she knows it's okay to be herself.

It's odd how I look so much into this, but I appreciate her so much, I guess I just value all the things she has brought along with her. She's my best friend, and I really do love her for that.

Gesturing for her to follow, I walked out of the foyer and over to the stairwell. Glancing back into the bag I wondered if I could somehow figure out where it was that Dakota was taking me judging by the selection of clothing that Brooklynn had brought with her. I know it would spoil the surprise and all, but I just really wanted to know. I was almost beside myself with anticipation.

I overturned the bag of clothes over my bed and watched as a bunch of colors and fabrics cascaded out of the bag and onto my striped lined sheets. I snatched up a black turtle neck, capped sleeve top as soon as it caught my eye.

"I love this," I said as I draped it across me as I stood in front of the mirror.

Wondering what other goodies she brought, I turned back to the bed and began shifting through all the clothes that had tumbled out of the bag. There was a soft yellow wrap top that caught my eye, but it was no match for the black turtle neck that I still had clutched in my hand.

Her voice interrupted my clothes frenzy, "These leggings will go so well with that top," when I looked over she was holding a pair of black leggings that she had taken from my closet.

I walked over to her and agreed that she was right. The leggings were black as well, "Won't it be too much black?" I asked her not wanting to look like I was showing up for a funeral instead of my date.

She paused for a second, her eyes drifted to a place over my shoulder before lighting up as she walked past me and over to my bed, "Not if you pair it with this."

In her hand was a really stunning, cream pea coat jacket with three pairs of black buttons down the middle in a uniformed line. It was simply gorgeous. I am so jealous of the fabulous clothes that this girl has, the thing is she'd rather let me wear them. Is there a reason for me not to love her even more? I think not.

Twenty minutes later found me in front of my mirror admiring the pretty girl that was staring back. I felt beautiful, donned in the outfit that we had picked out and the loose, but sophisticated bun that Brooklynn had styled my hair in and the only make up I had on was a bit of mascara and a dab of sheer lip gloss.

"Thanks so much, but you still haven't told me where it is that he's taking me to, Brook," I mentioned turning to face her, sitting on my bed.

"You're welcome, and I don't plan on telling you. Why can't you just sit tight and let the boy surprise you?" she asked with a playful roll of her eyes.

"Why can't you just tell me?" I asked knowing that it was a lost cause.

"Not happening," she said, "Now, he's coming to pick you up in a few minutes, do you have everything?"

"Purse, check, lip gloss, check, mints, check, any idea of where I'm going tonight . . . nope," I tried again.

"You will not give up, will you?" she asked with a laugh.

"My name wouldn't be Jamie Austin if I did," I answered proudly.

"And if I told you, Dakota would kill me," she responded.

"Hmm . . . you make a good point. I do need you to be there to squeeze my hand when I'm giving birth," I said seriously.

"And I will be if you stop asking about your date," she replied with a smile.

Brooklynn's P.O.V

I could tell she was going to have a blast. If the smile on her face when Dakota rang the doorbell was any indication, then there was no doubt that Jamie would enjoy herself tonight.

I, on the other hand had no idea as to what I was supposed to do to occupy the rest of my time. I was currently sitting in the Austin's den wondering how I was supposed to spend the rest of my night until Jamie came back.

It's weird how you can wake up and not even know that you had fallen asleep. It's one of those feelings that normally get brushed off easily without a second thought though. It's obvious that I must have nodded off on the couch in the den so there was no need to panic. It's not like I woke up in a different place or anything to cause alarm.

The television was still on, though it was now on another sitcom. I wondered how long I was asleep. I sat up and looked at my watch in the dim lighting. It was too dark to determine the figures on my watch so I stood and made my way over to the light switch to flip it on, but before I could check the time like I was intending to do, a loud peal reverberated throughout the house. For a moment or two I was a prisoner to confusion as I tried to figure out what could have made that sound. Then it became obvious that someone was at the door.

Halfway to the door I began to single out the possible candidates that could be at the door. Tammy was at her night shift at work so it couldn't be her and it was still too early for Jamie to be back from her date. When Jamie left she didn't say anything about anyone coming by and she informed me that her mom always calls if she's coming home early. I tiptoed so I could see through the convenient peephole that was located near the top of the door.

I was more than surprised to see Ajay standing on the other side. I unlocked and opened the door, quickly ushering him inside and out from the biting cold. He welcomed the gesture, moving quickly inside and removing the hood of his hoodie.

"What are you doing here? Jamie left on her date with Dakota like," I paused, checking my watch finally, "two hours ago," I informed him thinking that he must have forgotten.

"I know," he said sticking his hands in the pockets of his sweatshirt.

I waited for a moment thinking that he was going to inform me about why he was here nonetheless. It never came so I ventured out and asked another, hoping to clear the confusion as to why he was here, "Then what are you doing here?" I asked.

"I was at your place and then when your mom told me you weren't home, I figured you'd be here," he bit his lip as he answered.

My mother had come home yesterday while I was at school and seeing that I spent the night at Jamie's, I couldn't have known until I went home today. She didn't ask about my whereabouts so I assumed she either; (a) didn't care or (b) didn't even notice I was gone.

"Well you guessed right, is something wrong?" I asked, worried that something must have happened.

He gave a reassuring smile as he answered, "No, everything's fine. I just thought that I'd come hang out with a friend seeing that it's a Friday night and we both have nothing to do."

I shifted my weight to one foot so that my hip was cocking out slightly with my arms crossed, "What makes you think I have nothing better to do?" I asked defensively.

He gave a small smirk indicated that he saw right through my façade—I mean he was right. I did have nothing better to do—but he decided to play along anyway, "I'm sorry, were you busy? I guess I can always go find someone else to hang out with," his lips quirked at the corners as he turned to leave.

I rolled my eyes as I dropped my defiant stance, "Ok fine, what did you have in mind?" I asked knowing that he wasn't going to leave anyway.

He turned back around with a cheeky smile as he addressed me, "I don't know, I was hoping we could figure that out together, my plan was just to find a friend; mission accomplished," he upturned his palms momentarily before letting his arms fall to his side, showing that was all he had to give.

I walked into the kitchen and sat myself at a bar stool; he followed my actions and sat next to me, placing his folded hands on the countertop before him. The room was enveloped in comfortable silence for a short while as we both pondered on the possibilities we had to choose from.

"We could always . . . nah," he said from my left.

I thought about all the things that we could do but came up blank. I didn't really go out on Friday nights. I didn't go out . . . ever. This whole friendship thing was bringing along a lot of firsts for me. I liked it.

It was strange how Ajay couldn't come up with anything to do, wasn't he always out and partying it up and having fun with friends? It should be easy for him to conjure up something to do.

"What's Tristan doing?" I asked as the thought of the overly hyper boy came to mind.

"Nothing that I know of . . . why?" he asked turning to face me.

"He seems like a bundle of energy, he'll probably be fun to hang out with, right?" I asked seeing that he was Ajay's best friend, he would know.

"Right . . ." he answered almost as if he was unsure.

"Then let's call him and see if he wants to hang out," I offered thinking that was a good idea.

"Um . . ." he seemed uncertain and I immediately condemned my idea.

"Sorry, I just thought that . . . never mind. What do you think we should do? What were you going to suggest before?" I asked.

"Why are you sorry? You're right we should call him, it's a great idea. And I didn't really come up with anything . . . I just said that so it would seem like I tried at least," he said sheepishly as he pulled out his phone.

I smiled in relief and amusement. I can't help the fact that I immediately jumped to conclusions all the time. He looked like he was going to snub the proposal leading me to think I had said something wrong or . . . I don't know. Like I said, this whole friendship/social skills thing is new to me and I am still getting used to it.

There was a silence before I heard him talk, "Hey man, you busy?"

I was surprised when I heard Tristan's voice filter clearly throughout the room, "No, why? What's up?" he asked.

The phone was on loud speaker, I realized, as Ajay set it on the counter and Tristan's voice resonated throughout the room.

"Well I'm here with Brooklynn and we—" he was cut off by Tristan.

"Oh, you are? Tell her I said hi!" he said and I couldn't help the giggle that tumbled out, this boy was just one of a kind.

"She can hear me? Hi Brooklynn, what's up? You're hanging out with Ajay and not me? I thought we were friends now? Don't you like me?" he asked leading me to look at the phone in wonder.

"Hi Tristan and yes I am. We are friends, you know that and of course I like you or else I wouldn't be asking you if you wanted to hang out tonight with Ajay and me," I replied trying to answer all his questions knowing he would be looking for a reply to them all.

"Really? Of course I wanna hang out with you guys. Where at?" he asked.

I looked up at Ajay signaling that he should answer that question since I didn't know where we were supposed to hang out. It would be rude to just invite people over to Tammy and Jamie's house without permission from them.

"My place," he said, then as an afterthought he added, "And this isn't a party Tristan, you and you alone," he warned.

"Sure thing," Tristan replied before there was a click signaling he had hung up.

Ajay flipped his phone shut and slipped it back into his pocket, "Well let's get going."

I slipped off my bar stool and ran upstairs into Jamie's room to retrieve my jacket. As I came back downstairs to see him waiting patiently in the foyer, I thought that I should at least leave a letter for Jamie letting her know where I would be just in case she got to thinking that I went home.

I decided to put it on the fridge knowing that she would definitely get it there, then, headed back out to meet Ajay. He opened the door and allowed me to go out first and then locked it before he too made his way outside.

"C'mon," he said loudly as it was not only freezing out but now also windy.

His hand rested on my back as he guided me to his car parked at the end of the pathway. He opened the door for me after unlocking the vehicle and made sure I was inside safely before closing the door and going around to his side where I had opened the door for him before he reached it.

"Thanks," he said getting into the car and starting it, making sure that the heat was all the way up.

The drive was all of fifteen minutes to his house. It was only half past eight and it was dark out already, it still takes me awhile to get used to the seasonal change and the shortened days thing.

"Are you hungry?" Ajay asked as he flipped the lights in the kitchen on.

"Just a little," I answered as I took off my jacket and placed it on the back of a bar stool.

"What do you want to eat?" he asked taking off his as well and draping it on the stool adjacent to my own.

"Um, what do you have?" I quizzed looking up at him as he stood on the other side of the counter in the kitchen.

"Well let's see," he said pushing off the counter and making his way over to the refrigerator. He pulled it open and I was surprised to see that it was fully stocked and not with the things that I'd expected an eighteen year old boy living on his own to have.

It wasn't a fridge full of microwavable dinners and beers, but had basic cooking ingredients and resembled one of those fridges in those dream kitchens you see on the Food Network that had almost every ingredient imaginable.

"Hmm, we could make Chicken Alfredo, Shrimp Linguini or Pot Roast or even Mac n' Cheese," he finished closing the fridge to look back at me.

I wasn't that hungry, we could make something less complicated and I'd be satisfied, "All that sounds really good, but how about we just stick to a grilled cheese sandwich or something," I suggested with a smile.

He bit his bottom lip in thought before replying, "Just a grilled cheese sandwich?" he asked.

I nodded, "Any kind of sandwich will do, what about you?" while placing my elbows on the countertop and resting my chin in my hand.

He made a movement signifying he was going to turn around but then apparently thought better and turned back to me letting out a sigh, "Yeah, sure. A sandwich is fine for me too," he stated.

I tilted my head to the side slightly as I took in his behavior. If he didn't want a sandwich he didn't have to eat it. It's not like I was forcing him to do anything. But the way he was acting suggested he had more to say.

After waiting for a while in silence as he bustled about the kitchen getting ingredients I decided to take it upon myself to ask him.

"If you don't want a sandwich you can go ahead and make whatever linguini Alfredo you wanted," I said looking to see his reaction.

He stopped and then turned to me leaning up against the cupboard with his hands behind him on the granite top supporting his weight, "I'm not all that hungry, I'm just disappointed that I won't get to prove to you that I can really cook," he said with a defeated sigh.

"I'll take your word for it," I smiled reassuringly.

"But it's not the same as being blown away with just one taste of one of my exemplary dishes, by the way its Chicken Alfredo and Shrimp Linguini," he said with a cute lopsided grin referring to my earlier mix-up.

"You're really confident about your culinary skills," I replied.

"I am," he nodded.

"Well in that case, I give you permission to work your awesome artwork on the sandwich that you're preparing," I told him leaning back in my seat.

"And it shall be the most awesome sandwich you will ever eat," he said with a satisfied smile turning back around and continuing to bustle around the kitchen picking up the ingredients he needed.

"I wanna eat an awesome sandwich too," said a voice from behind me.

I nearly fell out of my chair at the sudden intrusion of the new voice. Nearly, but I did yelp involuntarily though. I spun around and saw Tristan smiling cheekily at me as he zipped down his hooded sweatshirt.

When the heck did he get here? I didn't even hear the front door open or close or any indication that another person was in the house until he decided to talk.

"Don't look so surprised, you knew I was coming," he said as he took a seat next to me.

"When did you get here? I didn't even hear anything. Were you planning on giving me a heart attack?" I asked looking over to see that he was wearing a bright blue shirt under his hoodie that made his eyes stand out more.

"Not really, but when the opportunity presented itself I just couldn't help it," he said with a mischief grin.

"Yeah well, you better watch your back from now on. It's not nice to be scared shitless like that. You'll see," I added a wicked smirk for the full effect and was rewarded with Tristan's smile slipping into an uneasy frown.

"Should I be worried?" he asked turning to Ajay but keeping his eyes on me.

The boy in question looked over his shoulder at us and then turned back to his work, "Maybe."

Tristan squinted his yes at me in some sort of evaluation for a few moments and then leaned back in his chair with a satisfied grin, "Nah, you're too nice to get me back. You don't scare me," he finished smugly as if he had me all figured out.

"So anyway, what are we doing tonight?" he spoke up, breaking our mini stare off.

"We don't know yet, that's why we called you over," Ajay said opening the fridge to get something out of it.

"Well let's see. After we eat our sandwiches of awesome then we can watch a movie, or play a game or we can spy on the next door neighbors because there is no way that those noises were normal Ajay. I don't care what you say, it sounds like a torture chamber over there," he said.

I gave him a look that clearly said how weird I perceived him to be. He was either used to the look or he simply didn't care—I think it's both—but he didn't seem fazed.

I turned just in time to see Ajay rolling his eyes at his best friend, "I swear to you they aren't torturing anyone in there Tristan," Ajay said.

"What makes you so sure?" he asked.

"I just know. Trust me," he replied.

"What are you talking about?" I asked though not sure I even wanted to know.

"My next door neighbors, well it's the husband actually. They're a married couple, and whenever the wife steps out for a while to go wherever it is she goes to, the husband stays at home and after a while there are always loud noises like people are screaming or moaning in pain," Ajay explained, "And Mr. I-watch-to-much-TV over there thinks that he hides captives in their basements and tortures them."

There was a moment of silence before I broke it with uncontrolled laughter. I couldn't help it. The story was just too funny and the looks upon their faces as it was being told was even more hilarious. My sides started to hurt and there was a shortage of air in my lungs. I probably looked like I was constipated or was being suffocated. Either way I knew it could not have been a pretty sight.

"Sorry," I breathed out as I regained my composure and sat up straighter in my chair.

"It's just that," I paused to take a deep breath to fill my deprived lungs, "you don't really believe that do you?" I asked addressing the both of them.

"No."

"Yes."

There was a silence again before I turned to Tristan, "Listen to yourself. There is no way that this guy could be torturing people in his basement guys. You're probably just exaggerating," I reasoned.

He shook his head, "I know what it is I hear Brooklynn, those noises are something to be suspicious of," he said right as a plate was placed in front of me.

I looked down to see a generously stacked sandwich. When I looked back up Ajay was coming back with two more plates. One which he placed in front of Tristan and one he took with him to his place on the left of Tristan at the last bar stool.

"Wow, this looks almost too good to eat. Do you have a name for such a masterpiece?" I teased as I brought the sandwich to my mouth.

Damn, he was right. This is by far the best sandwich I have ever tasted. What did he put in here?

I tasted chicken first and foremost, then there was cheese and a delicious blend of sauces and lettuce and tomatoes and . . . . this was amazingly good.

"Chicken Teriyaki on Parmesan Oregano bread," he said like it was the most obvious thing in the world, because I, of course, conjure up gourmet sandwiches in my kitchen all the time . . .

As I took another bite of my new found heaven I wondered how kickass it would be if he started his own bistro and all he made were sandwiches like this.

He would get millions; he could even start a franchise and have—wait. Chicken Teriyaki . . .

"You stole Subway's recipe?" I asked skeptically.

"Of course not. I made it better," he said with a cocky grin before sinking his teeth into his own sandwich.

I rolled my eyes but didn't protest as it would mean I would have to stop eating and there was no way I was going to do that. I'll give him that. He did make it better, way better.

We did as Tristan planned; we watched a movie and even played a game of 'Uno' that I won on all four rounds. Although it was mainly due to the fact that I cheated, which they figured out by the middle of the second game, but they couldn't prove it or find out how. And they never will.

Midway through the argument that started about how I won all four games, there was an eerie noise that suddenly came to our attention. Needless to say, the topic of my suspicious winnings was forgotten and instead focus placed on the suspicious noise that we had all heard.

The silence was infiltrated by that noise once more.

What the hell was that?

My brows creased in confusion. Was that a person . . . moaning? My eyes snapped to Tristan and Ajay just as theirs snapped to mine and each other. So I guess it was safe to assume that we were all thinking along the same lines.

That's not normal.

We sat there for maybe a full three minutes before Tristan stood and said, "Now do you believe me?"

I looked to Ajay then up at him before answering, "Ok that was weird, but I still don't think anyone is torturing anyone," I said firmly.

Ajay then stood up too, "I agree, but that was a little too weird for me," he said.

I looked at the both of them as they towered over me, "What, are you scared?" I asked smirking from my place on the carpeted floor.

"No, I'm curious. We're going to find out what's making that noise once and for all," he said gesturing to me.

Now *I* was scared. They weren't really going to try and find out, were they?

And what did he mean by 'we'? I'm not curious nor do I have any intention of finding out the cause of the weird and suspicious noises. And there it was again, that ghostly moan. It was creepy.

I took his outstretched hand anyway and let him hoist me to my feet, "You're kidding right?"

His shaking head answered my question.

"We can't do that. That's considered spying!" I said trying to reason.

"No it's not; we're merely observing the activities of Ajay's suspicious next door neighbor without getting caught," he provided with a mischievous grin.

I gave him a pointed stare, "You cannot be serious. What if you do get caught?"

"We won't. Now put on your sweater and come on," Ajay said taking his, as well as my own sweater, off of its stools.

He handed me mine as he slipped his own on. Tristan merely zipped his own up since he had never taken it off to begin with.

I looked at the article of clothing in my hand and then at them, "Guys, it's almost midnight and it's freezing out, you have to be kidding right?" I tried to change their minds even though I found myself slipping into my jacket.

"We don't need flashlights, we can see clearly out there, my lights are on and so are his," Ajay spoke as he led the way to the foyer.

"Not the point!" I muttered as I followed next to Tristan.

It didn't take long for my fingers to start turning numb with cold as I followed silently behind Ajay, with Tristan behind me, "Where are we going?" I asked.

"To look through his basement windows," Ajay responded over his shoulder.

I almost fell over him as he suddenly bent down devoid of any warning. I glanced down to see him lying on his stomach with his head turned towards the faint light that was emitting from the small window that led to the basement.

"What do you see?" asked an eager Tristan.

"Nothing," Ajay replied.

"What do you mean, 'nothing'? Is anyone down there at all?" Tristan asked.

"No, you can look for yourself if you wanna. There is no one down there, just a couch and a TV," he said as he exchanged places with Tristan.

"Aw man," he said with a tone of disappointment realizing that he was in fact wrong with his far-fetched accusations.

"See?" I said trying to prevent myself from rolling my eyes.

He pushed off the ground and stood on his feet after regaining his balance, "So what, it's not in the basement. But we all heard those noises, something weird is going on here and you know it," he finished and as if to punctuate the sentence, there was that noise yet again, but it was louder and a little more distinct this time. For one, I could tell that the voice belonged to a man and it sounded as if he were in severe pain.

All heads turned to the illuminated window above us. So it was coming from upstairs. I looked back down to notice two pairs of eyes staring intently at me for some reason.

"What?" I asked, very doubtful that I would like their response.

"We'll give you a boost. C'mon," Ajay said with a serious face.

There was no way . . .

"What?! Are you crazy? No way!" I said shaking my head vehemently as I made to budge past them, but they moved to block me.

"Please Brooklynn, you're the lightest one, and you're shorter; let us boost you up so you can look through the window and see what's going on," Tristan tried to persuade me.

I stared wide-eyed at them, but they were serious and weren't going to back down. I had no choice but to accept my fate, however that didn't mean I had to like it. I grumbled under my breath about how stupid this all was and if I got caught they were going down with me.

Both their faces broke out in satisfied grins as they saw my compliance. They then proceeded to link their hands together and crouch down.

"Put your foot here and we'll boost you up," Ajay said motioning to their interlocked fingers.

"You had better not drop me," I said knowing that they wouldn't, but I was still paranoid about the whole thing.

"We won't" they responded simultaneously as I placed my right, Airwalk clad foot into their hands.

I was facing the wall as I stepped into their grasp so I braced myself against the flat surface as I felt myself being elevated. The window was still a foot or so above me and there was no way I could tip toe to peek inside, so with a look of mock disappointment I looked down at them, "Oh well, looks like I'm too short."

Before I could protest though, each had taken one of my slipper-clad feet into their cupped hands and raised their arms over their heads sending me up again about a foot up in the air to give me a perfect view into the room.

I almost screamed at the sudden movement and the new height I found myself at. My fingers tightly gripped the window sill as I said a short prayer to let me make it out of this alive.

"Look into the room and tell us what you see," Ajay said projecting his voice up at me.

I opened my tightly shut eyes and examined the room. The curtains were drawn, but they were sheer and beige so it was easy to see everything with the aid of the lights that were on in the room.

It was a bedroom, probably the master, because there was a huge bed off to the next side. Wait. What's on the bed? I squinted with my eyes and tried to distinguish the mass that was draped over the bed.

There was movement and it became clear that someone was on the bed and on closer inspection it was a man . . . who was tied up. Why was he tied up? And why was he not wearing any clothes besides a pair of skin tight Speedos.

What kind of sick torture is this?

"What do you see?" Tristan asked and I was about to tell him that he was right about his suspicions when another figure walked into the room.

I ducked my head a little so as to eliminate the possibility of him seeing me. He said something but I couldn't hear it so I depended on my eyes instead. And the sight I saw just kept getting weirder and weirder.

The guy that had just entered was wearing a tight, black, latex suit similar to Halle Berry's costume in her movie 'Cat Woman'.

What the . . . ?!

There was more muffled talking and then the noise that triggered our whole spying escapade sounded again. But the thing is, Speedo Guy wasn't moaning nor was he in pain, well at least I hope not. It appeared that he was doing a bad impersonation of a . . . cat?

This makes no sense!

"Come now kitty, drink up!" that was the first thing I could actually hear in the muffled words that were said so far.

The Cat Man then proceeded to place a bowl of what I assumed to be milk on the floor. Speedo Guy then did that horrible meowing sound again as he shuffled off the bed and slid to the floor where the bowl of milk was and started lapping it up. Literally.

What the . . .?

After he had lapped up his fill, Cat Man bent to pick up the bowl, but Speedo hissed and scratched him on his leg. The next few seconds happened too fast for me to make any sense of it all.

Cat Man with a sudden rage took up the bowl and flung it across the room. Guess where it happened to hit? The window; there was a loud shatter of broken ceramic and a splash of white as it smashed right in front my unsuspecting face. Then, all of sudden I had lost my balance and my hands were no longer gripping the window sill, but flailing around, madly trying to hold onto something to stop myself from falling. Too late. There was a rush of air, then a rush of pain.

I saw stars. Then my senses came back and I figured I had fallen from a height of two floors and it hurt. Though as I lay there and assessed the pain, I figured it didn't hurt as much as I would expect the impact from a fall like that to hurt.

The ground, at that moment, moved beneath me.

Huh?

It took me a long moment to come to terms that it wasn't the ground but the bodies of the two guys I had fallen on. I was still for only a moment longer before I pulled myself to my feet and off of them. Ajay sat up first and I breathed a sigh of relief that I hadn't killed him and another one made its way out as Tristan too sat up.

"What happened? What'd you see?" Ajay asked as I helped him up.

"I'm not exactly sure," I responded as I helped Tristan up too. I looked up at the window and made out the movement of faint shadows, "Let's go inside before they see us."

"They?" Tristan quizzed as we all made our way hurriedly back into Ajay's house where the warmth welcomed us graciously.

I walked over to the plush couch and let my frame sink into its embrace with a long sigh. They took their places on the floor in front of me, eager to know what I had seen.

I opened my eyes a few seconds later to see them sitting before me, ready to hear everything I had just been unfortunate enough to witness. I still couldn't make sense of what I had seen. I'm pretty sure I didn't want to make sense of it either way. That was just something in life that I never want to relive again. That was an epic 'WTF' moment.

"I . . . wow," I muttered, having nothing better to offer.

Still they waited for more. I prepped myself for the inevitable. They'd ask and ask until I spilled anyway so might as well save myself the headache and tell them now.

"You just would not believe," I said looking down at them as they sat before me.

"Tell us anyway, was he torturing someone up there?" Tristan asked.

The only person that went through any torture was me

"Not exactly," I answered truthfully, because I honestly did not know what went on in that bedroom.

"Stop the suspense and tell us already," Tristan snapped so I did.

I told them exactly what I saw and how I saw it and left them to make their own sense of it and by the looks on their faces, they were in the same position I was in. We were all sitting in silence warped in our own imaginations of the twisted things we had just learned. Tristan sighed, and then I shuffled around on the couch for a bit. Ajay proceeded to scratch his nose. The silence ensued, but it came to an end when I decided that was enough thinking for one night.

"Ok, so Ajay's neighbor is a role playing freak. I'm a champion at Uno, either that, or you guys just suck and Ajay puts the awesome in the most awesome sandwich I have ever tasted. I say this evening has been eventful," I stated cutting the silence.

"I always knew he was a weirdo, you cheated although I have no idea how and everyone whose anyone knows my sandwiches are awesome, so all in all; I say we really haven't done that much," Ajay followed with his reply.

"I don't need to cheat, you're just a sore loser," I smiled innocently.

"He's right, you cheated, but that's a conversation for another time. What do we do now?" Tristan asked looking back and forth between the both of us.

I turned and gave him a look clearly indicating my uncertainty. What does he mean, 'what now'? It's half past midnight. What else is there to do?

"We can't call it a night yet, I'm not even sleepy!" he stated.

"We've basically done everything under the moon and then some. You still want more?" I asked incredulously.

"Not everything," he said in a child like voice.

I rolled my eyes knowing he would take it literally. But before I could tell him I was out of ideas my pocket vibrated. I jumped slightly not at all expecting the sudden feeling. Reaching in my back jeans pocket I slipped out my phone, and answered it, "Hey Jamie," I greeted.

I didn't need to look at caller ID to know that it was her calling. The only two people that had my number were her and my mother. Chances are the caller was Jamie.

"Hey, I got your letter. I just came back from the gallery," she told me and I could hear the sheer joy in her voice. I knew Dakota would give her a great time.

"Good to hear, did you guys have fun?" I asked already knowing the answer.

"It was amazing. We even got to meet with a few of the artists. They were there since it was opening night and all, and let me tell you Brook, their paintings were fabulous!" she gushed and I couldn't help the smile that broke out.

"Well I'm glad you had fun," I told her.

"Me too, and thanks for not telling me. The surprise was really worth the wait and suspense," she stated what I already knew, "How was your night?"

"Well, that's a conversation that would be best held in person, but I did have fun so that makes the two of us," I answered.

"Great, well I'll call you tomorrow okay?" she offered and I accepted.

"Yea, of course. Goodnight Jamie."

"Night," was followed by a click signaling the end of our conversation.

"I wasn't aware that you had a phone," I heard as I slipped the contraption back into my pocket.

I turned my attention to the two boys occupying the space I was previously sitting in.

"Oh um, well you know now, I guess," I said airily as I sat on the other side of Ajay.

"Well wanna give me your number so we can text and all that good stuff?" Tristan asked.

I slipped my phone out and held it out to him, "Sure."

I got two phones back in return. Both Ajay and Tristan had supplied me with their phones in anticipation that I would save my number in them. I did while they proceeded to do the same to mine.

As my phone was handed back to me Ajay informed me that he had put Dakota's number in there as well.

I don't know if this makes me sound odd and neither do I care, but the fact that we just did that symbolized in a way that I was a part of this group of friends now. That I belonged and I was wanted. It's a very nice feeling, I said to myself.

Life has been looking up for me lately. I'd been making friends and best friends, sharing and keeping secrets and feeling a sense of belonging. I felt happy and welcomed and worthwhile.

November 25—Saturday

I woke up in my own bed, to the sound of my own alarm clock blaring Saturday morning tunes from the radio and glanced up to see my mother's eyes staring back at me from the doorway.

I blinked a couple of times and then sat up to face her.

Why is she just standing there?

I waited for her to say something or do something but she just stood there and if she continued doing that any longer I would have been worried, but as if reading my mind she chose to speak at that moment.

"Get ready, we're going to Mom and Dad's," she said.

It looked as though she was about to say more but she closed her mouth as if thinking better of it and left. It took me a moment to register what she just said because I was still puzzled about the whole encounter.

"Okay," I mumbled to myself as I pulled off my covers and slid off my bed.

I went straight to my bathroom to get ready. No hesitation whatsoever because if it's one place I'd always be willing to go is my Grandparent's place. Just the thought of Grammy's loving face and Jo Jo's soothing voice brought a smile to my sleepy face. They were the only two people I loved with everything in me because they were probably the only two people who loved me back at all.

They had taken care of me when my mother was too busy building her career to care. They were the ones who hired nannies to take care of me when my mother suggested giving me up for adoption. They always sent me birthday cards and get well soon cards when I had the flu. During the period where I was old enough to not require a nanny and too young to stay at home alone, they were always willing to take me in when my mother went on her long 'business trips', but as I grew older and gained the independence to be able to stay home by myself, visits became less frequent. I still kept in contact with them though, but I hadn't seen them in over a year.

I loved it there too. From what I can remember their house was always filled with playthings to keep me occupied and content. Every time I came over they always had new toys waiting for me. They were always willing to take me to the park and for ice cream, even though they had a 24 hour live in cook and the closest public park or ice cream shop was some way off. But that didn't matter. They wanted me to have a happy childhood rich with happy memories. I will forever be grateful to them for providing me with just that and so much more.

Just as I had finished changing, my phone gave a beep from my night table signaling that I had just gotten a text. I picked it up on my way to the door and read the message.

"Just thought I'd let you know that I'm going to the doctor's today for an appointment so I'll call you after."

I smiled vaguely at the message on the screen. Every time the baby was mentioned I felt just a little happier inside. I couldn't wait for his arrival. Just the thought of him was uplifting. Jamie was nearly three months pregnant though. The ninth of next month would make it three. Not even halfway there, but it's like I couldn't wait. Her due date is in May, but ever since I found out about her pregnancy I couldn't help but feel connected to her and her child in some way.

Maybe it was the whole coincidental thing where my mother was in her place 16 years ago and I was in the baby's place, but there was no denying it that I felt a connection to the both of them. I couldn't explain it, but it was there.

I sent back a message letting her know that I would be out of town visiting my grandparents for the day in case she decided to stop by and I wasn't home.

"Brooklynn," my mother's voice rang out.

"Yes," I answered as my foot hit the bottom stair.

"Ready?" she asked.

I wondered for a moment or two why she even bothered asking. Normally when I went anywhere with her she would act as if I wasn't there until necessary, not that I normally went anywhere with her. I brushed it off though.

"Yes," I replied as I walked into the kitchen to see her sitting at the island.

I went straight over to the fridge to grab something to snack on until we arrived at Grammy's and JoJo's. It was an hour long drive from where we lived. They lived on the outskirts of the next town over on a wide acreage of rolling green hills that their vineyard occupied. It was beautiful and peaceful because their next door neighbor was approximately a mile and a half away.

I snatched an apple and a bottle of water knowing that when we arrived, Grammy would have the table laden with all of my favorite breakfast foods. I took a bite out of the apple and waited for my mother to show that she was ready.

She stood from her seat, swiped her keys from the counter and made her way through the door to the garage on the other side of the room. I followed and waited for her to open the car.

The lights on the farthest vehicle flashed and I assumed she felt like taking the Lexus today. Normally she took her Audi whenever she went anywhere. I don't know what compelled her to take the SUV. Maybe it's because she didn't want me in her favorite car, but whatever the reason I wasn't complaining because this car was my favorite. JoJo bought it for her on her birthday but I was the one to choose it. I doubt she knew that though.

It was so pretty, with its glossy white paint job shining under the florescent show lights and the interior was beige and sleek. I was only twelve at the time, but if I had to do it again my choice would still be the same.

The garage door opened, illuminating the entire garage before we sped out and began the drive to the place I truly considered to be my home.

"Grammy!" I shouted as I literally leaped out of the car at the sight of my grandmother stepping off the patio to come greet us.

Her eyes lit up in reaction as she saw me running over to her. The light wrinkles around her eyes added to her soft and tender nature. Her arms were stretched open in anticipation of a hug. The feeling as they closed around me, when I softly barreled into her, was the greatest feeling ever. This was home. This was where I was comfortable and where I knew I was loved.

"How have you been, miele?" she asked me as we pulled apart.

"I've made some new friends and I really love them, they're great. How are you?" I asked.

"I've been enjoying all life has to offer, but now that my grandbaby is here life just got a whole lot better," she said patting my cheek, her Italian accent shining through.

Even after all these years in America and marrying an English man she still sometimes speaks in her native tongue. Speaking of that man, I saw my grandfather stepping out of the house.

My smile broadened as I caught sight of him. I kissed my grandmother on her cheek and then scurried over to the greatest man in my life, "JoJo!" I squealed as I threw myself into his arms.

He still smelled of cinnamon and sandalwood. A scent I had gotten so used to over the years in my life. The scent that brought back memories of playing hide and seek in the vineyard and bed time stories, all of which he was a part of.

"How's my favorite granddaughter?" he asked with a wink as he embraced me.

"I'm great. How're you? Holding down the fort without me?" I asked referring to the imaginary fortress we had.

"Barely, but I'm managing," he said as he let me go to hold me at arm's length, "You've grown some, haven't you?"

"From last year Christmas, I'd hope so," I recalled.

His face fell into a slight frown, "It's been that long since I've last seen you, huh?" he stated sadly.

I nodded.

"Christine, why has it been so long since I've seen you two?" he asked looking over my head at my approaching mother.

"I've been busy Dad," she said.

"Too busy to see your parents?" Grammy asked pulling her daughter in for a hug.

"Never" she replied as she sunk into her embrace.

I looked on with a bittersweet smile as I saw my mother hugging her mother. I turned around to JoJo who told me that breakfast was waiting. I nodded and went inside to wash up, feeling the onset of hunger coming on as the most delicious smells wafted through the foyer towards me.

We were all seated around the table and everyone was engaged in comfortable chit chat. That is until my phone rang and I excused myself from the table to take the call.

I flipped it open without looking at the caller ID status and answered, "Hello."

"Jamie's in the hospital," came from the other end.

My face fell, "What?"